AN EMERALD COVE CHRISTMAS

CHRISTMAS

EMERALD COVE

LILLY MIRREN

black lab press

WELCOME TO EMERALD COVE

Read the series in order...

Cottage on Oceanview Lane
Seaside Manor Bed & Breakfast
Bungalow on Pelican Way
Chalet on Cliffside Drive
Christmas in Emerald Cove

CHAPTER 1

ADELE

20TH DECEMBER

*S*he didn't see the seagull at first. Adele Flannigan's mind was elsewhere, thinking through what she'd need to do the moment she walked through the doors of the cafe. Wondering whether they had enough supplies to weather the rush of tourists that shouldn't have surprised her, but somehow had, given that it was her first time managing the cafe during a major holiday.

She tucked a stray strand of blonde hair behind her ear and smoothed her ponytail as she crossed the street, her bike rolling along beside her. Then she noticed the bird. It squatted on the footpath ahead of her, one wing slightly outstretched, it's beak ajar as though it was panting.

With a frown, she paused, studying the seagull. "What's going on little buddy?"

The bird didn't move. It lolled on one side, looking decidedly stunned. With a deep breath, she rolled the bike around the bird to the bike rack and padlocked it. Then she returned to look at the seagull again. She had a million things to do, and she'd be running late if she didn't hurry to open the cafe for the staff. But still, she couldn't walk away and leave it. What if it was injured or sick? It was so close to the road and vulnerable where it lay out in the open.

She squatted beside it, squinting into the morning sunshine that glanced off the roof of the Foodstore across the street, almost blinding her. She sheltered her eyes with one hand. "What am I going to do with you?"

The bird stared at her out of one black beady eye, then turned its head to watch her from the other eye.

"Did you run into a window or something? Did a cat get you? I wish I knew what was wrong, so I could help you," she whispered.

A quick glance up and down the main street of Emerald Cove revealed there was no one else around at that time of the morning, other than an occasional passing car. The Foodstore was still shut, and the pharmacy was as well. The Chinese Garden wouldn't open for hours yet. And the Surf Life Savers hadn't set up on the nearby beach yet either. The club appeared empty.

She reached out a hand and cupped the bird's back. It shuffled forward a little, so she retracted her hand and sighed. "Should I take you to the vet?" If she did, she'd be unbelievably late, and the entire day would be knocked off course. There was a lot going on at the cafe — she still hadn't gotten used to the ordering process. Mum had done everything on paper, over the phone, and using her experience to guess quantities.

Adele had gradually transferred all of the stock, vendors, and ordering information into a brand new piece of software she'd purchased, but it'd take time before it all worked smoothly. So far, she was a little behind on orders. And on top of all of that, she was having continual issues with staffing. Staff not showing up for their shifts, or leaving early, or forgetting to let her know when they weren't available, and the constant bickering between them all was becoming overwhelming.

"Wait right here, I'll get you a box or something, and maybe some water," she said.

She jogged around to the cafe's front door and found Crystal Waters leaning against the wall, inspecting her fingernails. Her long, black hair obscured her face.

"Hi, Crystal," said Adele. "Sorry, I'm a little late."

Crystal smiled. "No worries."

Adele unlocked the door and let Crystal in, then followed her, veering off to the kitchen to look for a small box and something to hold water for the bird. Before long, she was outside again, scurrying to where she'd last seen it. It was still there but flapped a little as she approached, and its beak was now shut.

She sat beside it, tried to feed it some water, but it didn't seem interested. Then, within a few minutes of her return, it suddenly righted itself, flapped its wings, then flapped again and leapt into the air. It flew towards the beach and joined the birds already circling high above the sand.

"Not even a goodbye, huh?" Adele watched it go, one hand cupped above her eyes. She smiled and stood to her feet, brushing the dust off her rear end.

Across the street, Marg waved to her as she opened the Foodstore. Nearby, a car pulled into a parking lot at the curb and a young man climbed out. He was well-dressed and had an athletic physique, his dark hair perfectly tousled. He was on the phone, talking quietly to someone when an elderly woman began fighting with a grocery trolley outside the

Foodstore, attempting to extract it from the line of trollies in the bay. The trolley wouldn't let go and the woman couldn't dislodge it, no matter how she tried. Adele was about to cross the street, when she saw the young man hang up the phone and jog up the ramp to help.

He tugged the trolley free, and the woman thanked him before walking into the shop. He spun around to walk back the way he'd come and for a single moment his gaze found Adele's. She was too far away to see the colour of his eyes, but she guessed they were dark brown. And as his eyes met hers, her heart skipped a beat.

Within moments he'd walked into the pharmacy and out of sight. Why did she never meet men like that? Handsome, put together, and kind to little old ladies when no one else was watching. Where were these men? Clearly, they existed, he was evidence of that, but she didn't seem to cross paths men like him. She'd thought her ex-boyfriend Antoine was a good guy the first time they'd flown together. It'd been a rural flight, only twenty passengers, and she was the co-pilot. He was handsome, confident, and when he'd flirted with her, she couldn't believe her luck.

With a sigh she retrieved the box and the dish filled with cool water and returned to the cafe. At least the seagull was okay, and she hadn't stashed it in a box — she honestly didn't know what she'd have done with it anyway now that the only vet she knew, her sister's friend, Vicky, had moved away from the Cove. With one last glance at the sky and the gulls that hung on the updraft overhead calling to one another, she stepped through the cafe's front door and steeled herself for the day ahead.

* * *

THE CRASH of waves in the distance was like a metronome, the rhythm a backdrop to the bustle and hum in the busy *Emerald Cafe*. Adele wiped her sweaty hands on the white apron tied neatly around her waist and studied the bookings in the ledger by the door. They'd be full that night. Crystal Waters, their resident musician, and a waitress at the cafe, was playing. She always drew a good local crowd. Besides, it was almost Christmas and Emerald Cove was full to the brim with summer tourists.

She tucked a stray strand of blonde hair behind one ear and moved the couple listed for table four to table eight. That way she could push table four up to table two and create enough room for the group of six who had a birthday booking.

Managing the cafe was taking more of her time, energy, and strength than she'd ever imagined it could. She'd helped Mum plenty of times over the years, working as a waitress or kitchen hand. She'd even taken a turn at cooking when the cook had called in sick a few times. Summers during her high school years had been spent right here, in the cafe, ferrying baskets of chips and chicken parmigiana to tables of tourists.

But managing the staff, supplies, and guests was an entirely different matter. And she loved it. The challenge of it, the busyness. The fact that there were regulars who came on the same day every week, whom she'd already grown to know and love. And the tourists who came once or twice, with their smiling red faces, stark tan lines, playful children, and insatiable appetites. She loved it all — yet she couldn't help wondering if she could manage this level of exhaustion long term.

"We're low on napkins!" called Crystal as she hurried past.

Adele frowned as she retreated to the kitchen. She'd

meant to call the laundry service about washing the napkins and tablecloths but had forgotten and now they couldn't do it until tomorrow. The small linen closet in the back of the kitchen was almost empty. How would they manage for the night? She ran fingers through her fringe and tightened her ponytail with a sigh. They'd have no tablecloths and nothing for guests to wipe their mouths with. Perhaps she wasn't cut out for managing a cafe after all. She should call Mum and tell her she'd changed her mind. She couldn't possibly accept the business her grandparents had handed down. It was too much responsibility, and she was only twenty-four years old.

She slumped into a nearby chair and rubbed her hands over her face. Her feet ached and she desperately needed a drink of water. But the lunch crowd had been particularly large, and she'd not had a chance to grab anything for herself.

In her pocket, her mobile phone played a familiar tune. She tugged it free and answered with another sigh.

"Hello?"

"Hi Adele, how's life in a small-town?" Her friend, Becky, from Darwin called her every now and then to encourage her to return to the northern city. They'd been neighbours with flats across the hall from one another. Becky was a primary school teacher and they'd bonded over their shared love of movie nights and popcorn.

"Life is good, busy but good. How about you? Sick of the heat yet?"

Becky groaned. "It's unbearable. How is it possible that I forget every year how bad it gets in summer? Why would anyone choose to live here? I can't leave home without a change of clothes in my shoulder bag. Thank goodness school is finished, I don't think I could take another day stuck to my chair in front of a class of sweaty children."

Adele laughed. "You're always trying to get me to move back, but this really isn't helping your cause."

"I take it back. You should stay in Emerald Cove. I feel like I'm living in an oven. I'll be staying inside for Christmas. Speaking of which, what time does your flight get in?"

Adele glanced at her watch. She should get started on the dinner preparation soon, or she'd be running behind schedule again. "I don't have the details in front of me. I'll call you later about it, okay."

"But you're still coming?"

"I'm still coming. And looking forward to it. We can spend Christmas Day in the swimming pool together."

Becky sighed. "That sounds perfect. We'll go to Mum and Dad's for lunch, and we can swim all afternoon. They have a really nice pool, it's huge and has plenty of shade. Mum makes a killer cocktail, as well. You're gonna love them."

Adele felt a little uncomfortable going to a stranger's house for Christmas. But Mum and Athol were headed to New Zealand to see Auntie Sharon and Uncle Bart. Sarah and Mick had their two-month-old baby, so no doubt they'd be completely occupied with him. And Ethan and Emily were traveling to Tasmania for the holidays with Diana. That left Adele at a loose end, and she hated to be a bother to anyone. So, when Becky invited her to spend Christmas with her family in Darwin, she'd hesitantly agreed.

Now, she was wondering whether it'd been a good idea. Perhaps she should've simply spent the day with Sarah, Mick, and baby Leo. It would be quiet, but at least she'd be with family.

"How's the cafe?" asked Becky.

Adele glanced around the busy kitchen. A kitchen hand banged and clanked dishes in the sink as he scrubbed them clean. The cook wiped down gleaming stainless-steel counters.

"It's good. I'm getting into the swing of things. It's a lot of hard work though. I'm exhausted all the time."

"I bet you are. Listen, if you haven't given up entirely on flying, that airline in Hong Kong got back to you. You told me to open the letter if I saw it, so I did. They'd like you to come into their Darwin office for an interview. Maybe you can do that while you're up here."

"Wow, okay thanks for letting me know. I wasn't expecting it, to be honest. I know how competitive those positions are."

"So, what do you think? Would you give up the beach cafe lifestyle to fly in Hong Kong?"

Adele didn't know what to think. She'd come to terms with her new life in the Cove and was even enjoying it. It was freeing to be her own boss, something she'd never really considered doing before. But she liked it. She could make her own decisions, didn't have anyone's life in her hands. Although she missed the feeling of being up high, the power of the airplane around her, the throttle in her hands. "I don't know. I feel as though I've only recently settled into my life here. And Mum really needs me at the cafe. But I don't want to give up on flying yet, either. Can you send me a photo of it? I'll have to think about it and give them a call."

"Sounds like you have a lot to consider in the next few days before you fly north. So, I hate to do this to you, but before you get here, there's something you should know," began Becky, her voice changing tone. "It's about Antoine."

Adele's heart skipped a beat. Antoine was her married ex. He'd hidden the fact that he had a wife until she'd already fallen in love with him. When the truth came out, he told her their marriage was over, that he loved Adele, and would do everything within his power to be with her. But every time he made the promise, she'd waited, and nothing had happened. He was separated from his wife now, but Adele had moved back to Emerald Cove and cut him out of her life. Or at least, she'd tried to. He still called her sometimes and begged her to come back to Darwin. He'd even offered to fly to the Gold Coast to meet her, but she'd put him off.

"What about him?" she asked.

Becky hesitated. "He and his wife are back together."

"What? How do you know that?"

"Everyone's talking about it. I had coffee with Eamon, that pilot you gave my number to. Do you remember? Thanks for that, by the way. He's a complete psychopath."

"Eamon? No he's not, he's really nice."

"Maybe not a psycho, but he still lives with his mother."

"Hey, I've been living with my mother until recently. It's perfectly normal for someone in their early twenties these days."

"Of course, it is, sweetie. You're right. I'm sorry, he's a very nice man, just not for me. Anyhow, apparently Antoine took his wife to the office with him, introduced her around and bragged about how happy they are."

Adele swallowed. "Eamon said that? That they were happy?"

"Mmmm…and there's something else. She's pregnant. Even has a bump."

Her pulse thudded in her throat. Pregnant? They were supposed to be separated. "But if she has a bump…"

"Yep. That means the baby's at least four or five months along. When was the last time you spoke to Antoine?"

"Last week. He called me to see if he could visit. Wanted me to spend the weekend with him in Surfer's Paradise."

"Wow," exclaimed Beck. "What a jerk."

"I said no. I mean, I'm not comfortable having a weekend away with him. He's still married, even if they are separated."

"Seems like they're very much together."

Adele shook her head slowly. He'd lied to her so many times and every time she'd fallen for it. "Right. You're right — they're together, they have been all along. I can't believe I was so gullible. Mum told me he was using me. Not in so many words, but I thought she was being unfair."

"Your Mum is smarter than you give her credit for," admitted Becky. "Look, I have to go. But we can talk more about this when you visit. We'll have an amazing time and forget all about Antoine and his perfect little family."

She hung up the phone. Christmas music sifted gently through the cafe's speaker system. It contrasted starkly with the tumult going on inside Adele's mind. She'd loved Antoine. He'd been her first love. She was young and naive when she travelled to Darwin. On her own for the first time, away from home. And he'd treated her with kindness and affection. He'd drawn her in slowly, bit by bit, until she'd loved him without realising it. To find out now that it'd all been a lie brought a pain to her chest that made it hard to breathe.

She pushed herself to her feet. There was too much work to do. She couldn't afford to waste time pining for a man who'd never really loved her. With a shake of her head she wiped her eyes dry and pushed through the swinging doors into the cafe. Her mother stood by the entrance, running a finger down the booking ledger.

"Mum," she said, striding to meet her. She threw her arms around her mother and buried her head in her warm, soft shoulder. Mum smelled of lavender and baby powder.

"Well, this is a nice welcome," said Mum, patting her back. "Is everything okay, love? You look a little red-eyed and disheveled."

Self-consciously, Adele smoothed the apron over her faded shorts, and tucked her oversized T-shirt into the waistband. It was just like Mum to point out that Adele didn't meet her expectations for presentation. She was never mean about it, but her comment was pointed, and Adele knew exactly what she meant by it. The truth was, she'd given up putting any effort into how she looked most days. She was busy, on her feet all day long and at night too. She didn't have time for personal grooming, nor did she have the money to go shopping. The cafe had absorbed every cent she'd made, although she could already tell the Christmas rush would help refill the coffers. But truthfully, it wasn't important to her. Or maybe the issue was that she was still feeling deflated after fleeing her affair in Darwin.

"Yes, completely fine. I might be disheveled, but I'm a busy woman. You know that. And I'm happy to see you, that's all." She stepped away, wiping her eyes again. "What are you doing here? Don't you have to pack or something?"

"I wanted to check in and make sure everything's okay. I've never left the cafe at Christmas time before, and I'm a little nervous about the whole thing."

"We'll be fine, Mum. Don't worry about it. I've got it all under control." She ushered her mother away from the bookings ledger and towards the door.

"Did you remember to call the laundry service? Because this is the busy season and if you run out of linens it'll be a disaster." Mum glanced over her shoulder as she shuffled out of the cafe.

"Of course, it's all handled." It wasn't handled. Not even close. But her mother didn't need to know that. If she understood just how behind Adele was on linens, supplies orders, and shift scheduling, she'd never go to New Zealand and see her sister for Christmas. She knew that if she told Mum what was going on, she'd cancel her trip, swoop in, and take care of everything. But that wouldn't be fair on her, considering she hadn't been able to relax over the Christmas holiday since…well, *ever*. As far as Adele could recall, her mother had always run the cafe and hosted Christmas at her house, every single year of Adele's life.

"Wait, stop pushing me out the door," objected Mum, hands raised.

Adele set her hands on her hips. "Sorry, but I don't want you worrying about this place. I'll take care of it, you should enjoy your trip."

"Who is that man over there? We don't really allow dogs…" Mum pointed back into the cafe.

Adele spun to face the outdoor seating area, eyes scanning. An elderly man leaned forward on a chair, feeding something to a small dog that stood on its hind legs begging. His white hair had been blown into a bouffant by the ocean breeze and he wore a festive Christmas shirt, buttoned slightly off kilter, with a pair of long, khaki pants. Black-rimmed spectacles perched on his nose.

"I don't know," replied Adele. "Maybe a tourist. We've had a lot of them through the cafe today."

"Maybe," agreed Mum. "But I've seen him around, I think. When I was shopping last week, and at the police station when I was…" She glanced at Adele, cheeks reddening. "Paying for that speeding ticket, I didn't tell you about."

"Mum, really? Another speeding ticket? You're gonna lose your license if you're not careful."

Mum waved a hand. "Pfft…they give them out like lollies. It's a travesty if you ask me. They could be out there, solving crimes and putting criminals behind bars. But no, they're stalking senior citizens who are driving slightly over the speed limit because they're running late to a Pilates class. A complete travesty."

Adele shook her head. "I don't know what we're going to do with you. You'll have to ask Athol to drive you everywhere. I suppose he won't mind."

"I'm not going to lose my license."

"Good. So, you've seen this guy around? Maybe he's moved to the Cove. I don't recognise him, so he can't have lived here long. His dog seems well behaved." The truth was, she hated the idea of telling a little old man that his dog couldn't stay in the cafe.

"Perhaps you're right. Okay, I'm leaving. There's no need to push. I'll go and pack my bag — will that make you happy?"

"Very happy," replied Adele.

"Bye then!"

Adele watched her mother leave, then let her gaze wander back to the old man in the corner. He'd stopped feeding the dog and was staring at something on the table — a book perhaps. He looked lonely, the corners of his mouth hanging low. There was something about the slouch of his shoulders that made her sorry for him. He glanced up and met her gaze, then waved her over with his fingertips.

She strode to his table. "Yes, sir, can I get you something?"

"I'd love some hot chips with gravy, please. And a pot of Earl Grey."

"Right away." She hesitated. "Have you moved to the Cove, or just visiting?"

He reached for the dog, which had settled into the chair beside him, and stroked the animal's head. "I moved here about a month ago." He had a soft accent she couldn't place.

"Well, it's lovely to meet you. I know all the locals, so I should introduce myself. I'm Adele, I own this cafe. Well, my mother does officially, but I run the place."

He smiled, the corners of his brown eyes crinkling. "A pleasure to meet you, Adele. I'm Samuel and this is Eddy." He pointed to the dog. It looked like a Fox Terrier, with short white fur and black spots.

"I see you're reading."

"Yes, a thriller," he replied, closing the book to show her the cover. "It's a little scary so I like to read it in public." He offered her a wink, then laughed at his own joke.

She grinned. "I do the same thing. I can't read thrillers alone in my house at night. I have to read them on the beach, or out in the open somewhere with the sun on my face."

"We are kindred spirits then," he replied, dipping his head.

"We are indeed. I'll get you those chips, Samuel."

As she walked away, she couldn't help wondering if he lived alone, or if he had someone to care for him. His shirt buttons were mismatched, and he had a walking cane leaning up against his chair. She hoped he had someone to go home to. There was something about him that piqued her interest — a melancholy that provoked a compassion deep inside of her. Perhaps it was, as he'd said, that they were kindred spirits.

Her telephone buzzed and she pulled it from her pocket and stared at the screen.

Antoine.

Her heart dropped into her stomach, and she held the phone to her chest. Her eyes squeezed shut for just a moment before she muted the phone and slipped it back into her pocket. She couldn't talk to him now, not after her conversation with Becky. He'd lied to her — he wasn't separated from his wife or headed for divorce. He was expecting their third child with her and parading her around the office to show off their wedded bliss. She'd been taken in and she had no intention of letting him do it again.

CHAPTER 2

CARLOS

"*M*r Ruiz, please take a seat. Mrs Goode will be with you shortly." The receptionist sat behind a long, white desk. She peered out at him through darkly lined eyes half-obscured by a blunt fringe. A set of headphones wound around her head and within moments she was talking to someone on the phone without changing her posture or indicating to him in any way that she was finished speaking to him.

With an awkward bob of the head, Carlos Ruiz sat on one of the half dozen chairs that lined the wall in the reception area. He linked his hands together and stared at the modern but completely unremarkable oil painting across from him.

His heart stuttered in his chest, and he breathed deeply in an attempt to calm his nerves. He'd applied at *Foster and Young* for a job as an assistant in their psychology program. As a PhD student, he was well on his way to becoming an organisational psychologist and hoped that the experience working for this corporate group would add to his resume, and his bank balance.

A woman walked through the door wearing a pair of white shorts and an aqua shirt. Her blue eyes caught his attention, as did her lithe physique and light tan. She peered at a piece of paper in one hand and held a paper bag high in the other as she approached the reception desk.

"I've got a delivery for a Karen Goode."

"Mrs Goode likes to collect her food deliveries in person. Just to make sure...you know?" replied the receptionist with a forced smile. "Please take a seat, she'll be with you soon."

The woman hesitated a moment, before spinning on her heel and finding a seat opposite Carlos. He nodded at her, and she offered him a tight smile. She stared at him for a moment as though she recognised him, then looked away. She seemed familiar to him too, but he couldn't place her. An image of her standing on the other side of the street in front of the grocery shop flashed across his mind. That's right, he'd spotted her early that morning on his way to pick up Tito's prescriptions at the pharmacy.

"I'm waiting for Karen Goode too," he said.

She sighed, meeting his gaze again. "I hope she doesn't take too long, or her toasted chicken sandwich will be cold."

"You're a delivery driver?" he asked.

She shook her head. "I run the Emerald Cafe, just down the street. I don't usually do the deliveries, but when you manage a business, you end up being responsible for everything."

"Sounds like a challenge."

"Yep. How about you?"

He shrugged. "I'm here for a part-time job."

"What doing?"

"Organisational psychology. At least I hope so. But at this

point, I'd probably settle for answering phones or making coffee." He laughed softly.

"You're a shrink?" she asked.

"Not exactly. I'm studying."

She nodded. "Seems like it would be interesting."

He couldn't tell whether she was being sarcastic or genuine. But there was something very attractive about the young woman across from him.

"It is. I love learning about people and helping them if I can."

She studied him with what seemed like a little more interest. "So, you live around here?"

He nodded. "A few streets over. I moved in about four weeks ago."

"Seems like a lot of people are moving to the Cove at the moment," she said. Then shrugged. "I've lived here my whole life. Well, except for a few years up in Darwin."

"It must've been a nice place to grow up," he replied.

"It was. I loved it — my whole family still lives here. Fair warning — when people move to the Cove they hardly ever leave." She laughed. "That sounds like a threat, but it's not. This place gets under your skin, and you discover nowhere else really feels like home."

He hoped she was right. He'd never felt that way before and longed for it. Maybe it was because his family moved so much. Or perhaps the fact that he'd never known his father, and his mother had died when he was young. He didn't have roots. Not the kind of roots other people seemed to have. He felt like a sailboat. Always traveling and being tossed about on powerful waves he couldn't control. A home where he could put his feet on solid ground was attractive to him in a way he couldn't fully understand, let alone explain. Maybe Emerald Cove would be that place for him. Although it was hard for him to imagine spending the rest of his life in this tiny beachside hamlet. He didn't know anyone, other than Tito. And he wasn't exactly the beach-going type.

"I like the sound of that," he said.

She smiled. "I hope you get settled and don't forget to stop by the Emerald Cafe sometime. We have really good food."

"I'll definitely do that."

Her blue eyes sparkled. "I'm not saying that because it's my cafe either. Although, I can't really be trusted, can I? A completely biased opinion, I'm afraid. But true, nonetheless."

Her rambling was cute, and her openness drew him in. He was about to say something else, hoping to extend their conversation or maybe discover her name, when he was distracted by movement from the corner of his eye. A well dressed woman emerged from her office and stood tapping an impatient foot as she exchanged words with the receptionist.

The young woman hurried to hand her the bag of food, then left the office. He watched her go, wishing he'd come up with something more interesting to talk about. Some way to connect with her. Loneliness circled overhead like a flock of crows looking for somewhere to land. He missed Sydney and his friends — the group he'd gone through his undergraduate program with were all either working or studying further at practices and universities around the city. They still got together every weekend and messaged him about it. But the messages had gotten fewer over the weeks since he'd moved, and he expected they'd dry up completely before long.

Long-distance romances were tricky, but long-distance friendships never lasted. At least, that was what he'd heard from Tito after they'd fled the drug wars in Colombia when his mother was pregnant with him. By the time Carlos was born, Tito said he had lost contact with most of his old friends. Carlos had reminded him that they couldn't stay in touch if they didn't want to be killed by the drug cartel, and Tito had admitted that was true. The few times they'd visited Columbia in recent years, Tito had marvelled at the way he and his old friends had picked up the pieces of their friendship. He'd declared that it was as though no time at all had passed. Carlos wasn't sure he had those types of friendships. He doubted they'd stand the test of time. His friends had the attention span of a gnat. And he was too much of an introvert to keep things going on his own.

With another sigh, deeper this time, he returned his attention to the painting on the wall. He stared at it without taking it in, his thoughts lingering over the recent move to Emerald Cove. It seemed like a nice enough town, but not exactly a hive of activity for people his age. He'd never surfed before in his life and growing up in the western suburbs of Sydney, he'd spent most of his younger years skateboarding or walking everywhere. He hadn't owned a car before either, but now that he'd followed his grandfather to this small beachside town, he had no choice. He had to drive to attend classes at the university in Coolangatta. So Tito had given him his old Holden ute, since, as he said, he didn't need it anymore. His new assisted living facility was within walking distance of the beach, the shops and anything else he needed or wanted to do. If there was an event on in Tweed Heads or Coolangatta, he could take the bus or Carlos could drive him. So, Carlos had the Holden and now he needed a job so he could afford petrol and rent for the room he lived in at the nearby boarding house.

"Mr Ruiz, you can go in now. Mrs Goode will see you," said the receptionist with a wave.

Carlos stood to his feet, tucked his resume under his arm, and swallowed, then marched down the hallway with resolve.

CHAPTER 3

ADELE

"I hate this," said Adele, rubbing both hands over her face.

Sarah stared at her across the kitchen bench, both eyebrows arched high. "You know what you have to do, I don't know why this is so hard for you." Her long, brown hair was pulled into a tight ponytail that bounced when she moved, and she wore yoga pants and a blue halter top.

"You don't?" Adele grimaced. "I loved him. I'm know you always fall in love with the most amazing guys, but it doesn't make breaking up any easier when he turns out to be a liar."

Sarah huffed. "My ex-fiancé wasn't exactly a prize catch."

"True," admitted Adele with a half-smile. "So maybe you get how I'm feeling, just a little bit."

Sarah shrugged. "I suppose so, but I'm still frustrated with you. I'm running on far too little sleep to be gracious right now."

Adele took a handful of grapes from the fruit bowl and popped them one by one into her mouth. Sarah placed some crackers and sliced cheese on a plate, then wandered from the kitchen with it.

"Come on, let's go and sit outside. It's hot as hades, but at least we won't wake the baby."

Adele grabbed her steaming hot cup of tea from the bench, and still chewing grapes, followed Sarah out onto the deck. They sat under a navy umbrella, faded to almost grey by the sun. Adele swatted at a fly as she took her seat.

"So, are you going to call him then?"

"Yes, I'm working up the courage."

"You came over here to do that…"

Adele sighed. "I know, I wanted you to be here with me, so I didn't back out. But now I feel like backing out."

Sarah laughed as she sliced off a piece of Brie and slathered it onto a cracker. "Fine by me. Do whatever you like."

"That's not what you're supposed to say. I came here so you could keep me accountable, force me to make the call and stand my ground."

Sarah's eyes sparkled. "I'm not your mother, you know."

"Could've fooled me," muttered Adele, reaching for a cracker.

"What's that supposed to mean?"

"Huh? Oh nothing. You were a little bit bossy when we were kids, that's all." Adele knew it would irritate Sarah to have the word bossy thrown in her face. She hated it when Adele called her that. But she couldn't help herself. She'd always gotten a little bit of perverse pleasure out of making her sister's face turn red. She didn't know why, exactly, only that it was fun. Although she'd been making an effort lately to do it less. After all, they were adults now, so she should probably act like one. At least some of the time.

"I. Am. Not. Bossy." Sarah fumed quietly.

A bee hummed close by. No doubt working over the rose bushes in the garden that Mum had left behind when she sold the house to Mick and Sarah. She'd prized those bushes, but Adele had noticed earlier that there were already weeds in the garden beds. Sarah didn't have the time or energy to maintain such a large and expansive garden now that she had Leo.

"Of course, you're not. I was only joking," Adele agreed, patting Sarah's hand. "So, are you going to make me call Antoine, or not?"

"You've *got* to call him," replied Sarah, her gaze steely once more. "If you don't, he'll ruin your life and you'll never learn how to stand up for yourself."

"You know, he never once did anything nice for me."

Sarah took a bite of cracker and cheese, chewed loudly. "Really?"

"Don't get me wrong, he was romantic, and told me I was beautiful. Things like that. But he didn't help me when I had to move to another flat. I had to do it all myself, because I couldn't afford to pay movers. I asked him to help, but he said he was busy."

Sarah took a sip of tea. "With his wife, no doubt."

"I know that now. Whenever I needed him, or if I was feeling low, he wasn't there for me. Last year I got a Christmas tree for the flat, and I thought it would be something fun we could do together. I asked him to come with me, and he said he trusted me to pick something nice."

"Wow, that's a terrible line," said Sarah.

"I know. I had to lug the tree up the stairs to my flat all by myself. I got splinters, a stitch in my side, and the tree was a complete mess by the time I made it."

Sarah seemed to push against a smile. "Well, it's all behind you now."

"True." Although Adele wasn't so sure. She lived in Emerald Cove now, but how had things really changed in any other way? She'd still be lugging a Christmas tree home on her own with no one to help her. A year had passed, and she was in the same place she was last year, apart from geography. Sarah was married and had a baby. She'd written a book and would be going on a book tour before long. What had Adele achieved? She'd broken up with a married man who'd lied to her continuously, quit her career, moved back home, and taken over her mother's cafe. Not exactly a stellar year. "I wish I had someone to help me pick out a Christmas tree and get it back to my flat. It's so lonely doing it on your own."

"You can skip the tree and just share ours," offered Sarah.

"It's not about the tree," admitted Adele. "It's another Christmas alone. Even when I was dating Antoine, when I came here for the holidays, I felt alone. I had this boyfriend, who I loved, but I couldn't spend Christmas with him because, I now know, he was with his real family." She pressed fingertips to her eyes. She couldn't cry, not with Sarah watching. She was over him. It was time to move on. Crying wouldn't change anything. "I mean, he never introduced me to his family. When I asked about his parents or his sister, he'd act like he was ashamed for them to meet me. Now I know why, of course, but for a long time it made me feel like his dirty little secret. Like there was something wrong with me."

"Don't let yourself spiral down that dark hole again," said Sarah, eying Adele with concern. "You talk yourself into it by thinking about all the bad things that happened, and next thing you know the world around you is completely dark, and you can't see the light anymore." Adele often forgot just how well her sister knew her.

She inhaled a deep breath. "You're right, I shouldn't do that. It's Christmas, and I'm home with all of you — I'm not alone. Leo is the most adorable nephew in the world. I have a lot to be grateful for."

"Yes, you do." Sarah smiled. "And I do as well. It's good for us both to remember that." She covered a yawn. "Even if it *is* hard sometimes."

Adele finished a mouthful of cracker and brie and washed it down with tea.

"So, that phone call?" prompted Sarah.

With a flutter of nerves in her gut, Adele pulled her mobile phone from her pocket and dialled. She didn't dare hesitate since any pause would give her time to question her resolve. She'd back down, as she always did, and put it off for another day. But Antoine had called her repeatedly in recent days. It was time to put an end to it all.

"Hello?" His voice on the end of the line was deep and soft, as though he was happy to hear from her.

"Hi, Antoine," she said, keeping a brisk sense of business in her tone.

"Hi, sweetie, how are you?"

She grimaced at his endearment. "I'm fine. Listen, you've got to stop calling me."

He paused before answering. "Why's that?"

"We broke up, Antoine. It's over between us. You have a wife, and from what I hear, she's pregnant."

He huffed. "Who told you that?"

All the wind drifted from Adele's sails, and she slumped forward, her chin resting on one upturned hand as she leaned on the timber outdoor table. "It doesn't matter. It's true, isn't it?"

"Yes, she's pregnant."

"So, why are you still calling me?" She felt tired all of a

sudden. Tired of his lies and his manipulation of her emotions.

"I miss you," he said.

"Stop saying things like that. You don't miss me because we were never really a couple. You lied to me. And I wouldn't have called you at all, but I want you to stop bothering me."

"Come on, sweetheart…"

"Don't sweetheart me," she snapped. Sarah nodded vigorously, her arms crossed over her chest, eyes flashing. Having her there helped Adele feel strong and full of resolve.

"But…"

"I don't want to hear it," she said, her voice trembling. "You need to stop calling me. It isn't right."

He laughed. "I get it, I've been a jerk. I shouldn't have treated you that way. You deserve better."

"Yes, I do deserve better. You lied to me, you cheated on your wife, and on me as well, really, and not only that, you've chased me out of my career which I loved. I don't want to talk to you ever again."

She ended the call, tapped until she found the block feature, then slammed the phone down on the table. With both hands pressed to her hair, she smoothed it back from her face sharply. It was done.

Sarah placed a hand on her shoulder. "Are you okay?"

Adele nodded, surprised that her eyes were still dry. Although her hands shook, she felt strangely calm.

Sarah picked up the phone. The screen was shattered from top to bottom.

"You were very impressive," she said. "And you stayed strong. But maybe next time, just hang up the phone rather than slam it down on the table like that."

Adele laughed. "I can't believe I did that." She stared at the phone screen. "It's completely ruined."

"I hope you ended the call first, or he's probably deaf."

"I really don't wish anything bad on him," said Adele through a fit of giggles. "But if he had a little bit of industrial deafness, just temporarily of course, I don't think I'd be upset about it."

They both burst into howls of laughter. Adele sobbed through the laughter, her throat aching.

CHAPTER 4

21ST DECEMBER

ADELE

*W*ith sweat dripping down the sides of her face, Adele wound up the windows on her green hatchback. The hot ocean breeze felt similar to the rush of wind when she opened the oven door in the cafe kitchen — it'd curled her eyelashes a few days earlier when she'd stood too close. She cranked up the air conditioning as she navigated the roundabout near the cafe and headed out of town. She'd finished her shift for the day and had spontaneously decided that now was the time to pick out her Christmas tree.

All her life, Mum and Dad had bought a tree from the lot near Kingscliff. But since she moved out of home five years earlier to become a pilot, she'd tried her best to conjure up the holiday spirit by buying a small tree for herself. Mum's

Christmas trees were legendary in Emerald Cove. Always perfectly decorated, she had the Christmas tree farmer set aside his tallest and best tree for her every year before the selection was picked over by the crowds. But Mum had let slip that she wasn't going to do that this year — instead, she'd selected a plastic tree from the shopping centre in Tweed Heads.

A plastic tree!

If the divorce hadn't been apocalyptic enough for their family, now Mum was decorating short, plastic Christmas trees and traveling to New Zealand for the holidays. Nothing about this year would be the same, and there was an emptiness mixed with a tinge of desperation inside her chest that was new.

The only thing to do was to find the perfect tree for her new flat — maybe it wouldn't be as tall as the one Mum usually set up, and maybe she didn't have enough baubles to cover it yet, since this was her first time decorating a standard-sized tree for the holidays — but it would be perfect, nonetheless. And the perfection of her tree would calm that sense of unease, that hollow feeling that made her throat ache whenever she thought about spending the holidays in Darwin without her family. She didn't want to think about it, about how lonely she'd feel. She would push those thoughts down and squash them to the very depths of her mind.

If she let herself think about the upcoming holiday in Darwin, she'd have to consider the possibility that she might very well run into Antoine and his postcard-worthy family, and quite possibly drink too much eggnog to compensate and end up sick, alone, and with a raging hangover in the hottest city in the country.

Fa la la la la, la la la la.

She bit back a sob, combined with a giggle. Then slowed as she neared the Christmas tree lot. There were still plenty of trees available, although obviously the best ones were already gone. But she wasn't about to let herself leap into a negative tailspin now. A positive attitude was what she needed. There was nothing wrong with her life. It was a fine life. She had her health, her family, and a wonderful business by the beach. It was true that she'd also had her heart broken, lost her career, and moved back to Emerald Cove with her tail between her legs — something she'd sworn she'd never do when she left. But that was all fine. She could deal with it day by day and still smile at the future.

She could. Really, she definitely could. Probably. Well, she could at least give it a try, anyway. Maybe not smile, but she could certainly muster up a grimace or a smirk.

She could smirk at the future.

With a sigh, she parked beside the lot and opened the door. The heat rushed back in, dissipating the air conditioning in a single moment, almost taking her breath away. The latest heatwave had crested at forty-two degrees Celsius around two o'clock that afternoon. Now it was five p.m. it should begin to cool soon. But the usual afternoon breeze hadn't washed in over the ocean yet, and the stifling heat hung like a blanket, suffocating the small coastal community. She wore her trademark shorts — this time they were green with a ragged fringe. Along with a T-shirt that was cropped to reveal a peek of flat stomach, and a pair of green thongs on her feet. Her hair was piled on top of her head in a messy bun — really the only way to wear it in the middle of summer.

The lot was busy, with several families perusing trees. Which meant that the farmer was otherwise occupied and not able to help her. His daughter stood at the cash register — a small table with a cash box, close to the parking lot. She looked about ten years old, so Adele figured she wouldn't be much help either. She'd have to pick the tree out herself and get it back to her car alone.

That was fine. She could manage it. After all, she was a strong, independent twenty-four-year-old woman who'd lived away from home for five years and built a career as a commercial pilot. She hadn't captained anything big yet, instead she'd always been the co-pilot, but she'd have done it before long if she'd remained in the profession. And if she was able to help land a plane with three hundred and fifty people on board, she could manage buying and setting up a Christmas tree on her own.

With a resolute toss of her head, she strode into the lot, up and down the aisles, studying each tree as she went. Some were too spindly, others too fat. Still others were all dried out by the heat and could be a fire hazard in her flat if she wasn't careful. She wanted something tall, green, and full. Something that looked and smelled like Christmas, to brighten up her home.

Ever since she moved out of Mum and Athol's place to rent a flat on her own, she'd felt a little more like herself. She was moving on with her life, establishing a plan for her future with the cafe and building friendships in the Cove. But she'd never really enjoyed living alone. In Darwin, she'd often had roommates. They'd come and gone, but at least she'd had company. In Emerald Cove, she was with people all day long and had family popping in to see her most evenings, unless she was out with them or her friends.

The perfect tree almost jumped out at her. She stopped suddenly, eyes wide, then circumnavigated it with slow, measured steps.

Yep. It was the one. There was no doubt about it. It was tall, magnificently so. Round and full, with lovely fresh green needles. It looked as though it'd only recently been felled. It wasn't dried out or brown. She grinned and hurried back to tell the girl.

The farmer's daughter was morose and barely said a word. She took Adele's payment and handed her a trolley. Adele pulled the trolley back to the tree. With her head cocked to one side, she decided that it would be best to pull the tree into the trolley, rather than lift it over her shoulder. It was heavier than she'd realised it would be, but with a few grunts and several splinters in her arm, she managed it. Then, she trundled back to her car with a smile of triumph on her face.

Closer to the parking lot, a sprinkler shot a spray of water over the Christmas trees stacked against a fence ready to be shipped out to customers. The ground was soaked, and mud puddles dotted Adele's path. She navigated her way around the first pothole, but the trolley got stuck in the second. She tugged and pulled, then spun to face backwards and leaned against the handle. To no avail. It wouldn't budge. She should've worn different shoes. Her thongs slipped and slid on the slick surface.

She turned back and set her eyes on the rear of her car, only a few metres away, judging the effort she'd need to make. Then she pulled with all her might. At that moment, the sprinkler spun back in her direction, shooting sprays of water over her head. Her hands, now wet, slipped on the trolley handle, and she fell backwards with a shout, landing on her rear in the middle of a puddle.

Muddy water splashed over her arms, legs, and face. She gasped, squeezing her eyes shut as the cold water soaked through her clothing. Gravel grazed her palms. She grimaced and pushed herself back to her feet then surveyed the damage. Blood trickled down the back of one leg and a small, mud-coated cut on one palm stung.

She swallowed back a sob as she wiped her hands down

the front of her shorts. This was supposed to be fun. She was grasping for some holiday spirit in the midst of everything else going on in her life. All she'd wanted to do was to prove to herself that she could celebrate Christmas as a fully capable adult with her own life, her own flat, and her very own Christmas tree.

Crying wouldn't help. It certainly wouldn't prove her independence. But it was all she wanted to do.

"Are you okay?" A man's voice broke through her self-pity.

She spun to face him, wiping the water from her cheeks with a dirty palm as she did.

"Uh, I think so."

It was him, the man from the psychologist's office. She'd met him when she'd delivered food to one of the staff there. He'd seemed nice and impossibly handsome with his deep brown eyes, perfectly groomed, almost black hair, fashionable clothing, and muscular physique. Normally his looks would've intimidated her, made her awkward and quiet, but there'd been something warm about him that'd set her immediately at ease while she waited with him. And now he was there, looking at her with concern in those deep brown eyes.

"I saw you fall. That looked painful."

She glanced down at her injuries. The blood had stopped flowing, but there were still a red line on one leg, mixed with muddy water and snaking down her skin.

"It's not too bad."

"They really shouldn't have the sprinkler set so close to the parking lot that it wets the customers."

She grimaced as the spray reached her again. The sprinkler continued on its trajectory. She raised her hands in the air, laughing as the desire to cry dissipated. She was ridiculous, and she no doubt looked crazy as well, but in that moment, all she could do was laugh. "I'm already soaked through, so I suppose a little more doesn't really hurt."

He grinned along with her and shook his head as the spray dropped onto his hair and darkened his shirt. "Can I help you get the tree to the car?"

"I'd love some help," she admitted.

"I'm Carlos," he said, as he picked up the trolley handle from where it'd fallen into a puddle.

"Adele," she replied, holding out a wet, muddy hand.

He shook her hand, still smiling. "It's nice to meet you, officially."

"You, too."

He tugged the trolley out of the puddle, then she guided him to where her car was parked. He glanced at the hatch-back, then at the tree.

"This is your car?"

She nodded, popped the boot open and searched beneath fabric shopping bags for the clean towel she always kept in a gym bag for trips to the gym.

"Um…I don't think this tree is going to fit."

She hesitated, then studied the tree and the boot of her tiny hatchback. "I didn't even think about that. The only thing going through my mind was that I had to find the perfect tree."

With a sigh, she wiped her legs and arms dry with the towel. "I feel like such an idiot."

"Does the seat fold forward?" he asked.

She hurried around to side of the car and opened the back door. Before long she found a lever and pressed it. The seats folded down with a thud. "Hurray! Apparently, they fold forward. I only bought this car recently, so I haven't figured it all out yet."

"It might fit now, although you won't be able to shut the

boot. Let's hope you can get it home without it falling onto the road. I've got a rope in my truck."

They manoeuvred the tree into the back of the car. The trunk and several of the lower branches stuck out. So, Carlos brought the rope from his truck and tied the tree in place, fastening the hatch down over it so that it wouldn't fly open when she drove.

"Thanks," said Adele, wiping the sweat from her brow when they were finished.

"You're welcome."

"I'll get this rope back to you."

He shrugged. "No need. You can keep it."

As he walked away, heading into the tree lot, she chewed her lower lip and wished she'd dressed in something nicer, or perhaps hadn't landed in a mud puddle before seeing him again. With her shirt soaked through and a bloody knee, she could only imagine how she looked to him. He wore jeans that fit his form perfectly, along with a soft, blue T-shirt. His hair was perfectly mussed, and his teeth gleamed white against his tanned skin. He leaned down to switch off the sprinkler as he passed it, then waved her goodbye.

With a sigh, she climbed into her car and studied her reflection in the rear vision mirror. Mud streaked her face, her blonde hair was matted against her head, and her eyes looked as though she'd been crying. She shook her head as she pulled the car out of the lot. At least he'd been there to help. She might've made a terrible impression, but she didn't know how she'd have managed without him. And now she had to figure out how to get the tree from the car, up three flights of stairs to her flat. Thank goodness she had a rope.

CHAPTER 5

CARLOS

*T*he tree stood tall and regal in the cozy living room. Tito sat in his armchair surveying Carlos's handiwork.

"It looks good." He gave a nod of approval and reached for his glasses, pushing them onto the bridge of his nose.

"Thanks, Tito." Carlos was still puffing slightly from the effort of bringing the tree into the ground floor unit at the assisted living facility. "You're sure they don't mind you having this here?"

Tito's nostrils flared. "I don't care if they do. This is my place, isn't it? I can have a tree if I want a tree."

Carlos raised his hands as if in surrender. "Of course. It's your place. You decide."

One thing he'd noticed about Tito over the years — the older he got, the feistier he became. It made Carlos laugh sometimes, but he'd never show that to his grandfather. He was a proud man who couldn't stand to be made fun of.

Carlos loved him more than anything else in the world. In fact, he didn't have anyone else. It was just the two of them now that Yaya was gone. She'd died the previous year. And after almost fifty years of marriage, Tito was lost without her.

Outside, a seagull called softly in the distance. The beach was close by. The sound of the wind buffeting the building was a constant backdrop. There was nothing Tito loved more than to take a stroll along the clifftops and follow the winding path down to the ocean. He'd take his fishing pole and spend the entire afternoon standing with bare feet in the sand, casting his line out beyond the curling waves. For that reason alone, Carlos was glad he'd moved. His grandfather had been wasting away in a small townhome in an overpopulated suburb in Sydney. And Carlos had hardly ever seen him with his busy schedule and the heinous traffic. Now, they spent a portion of every day together as well as their weekends. They were a family again, even if it was only the two of them.

"You have to leave the angel until last. That's what Yaya always did," said Tito, rocking his chair back and forth.

Carlos nodded. "Okay."

This would be their first Christmas without his grandmother. Their first Christmas decorating the tree alone, just the two of them. At first, he'd considered not getting a tree. After all, it was only him and Tito. What did it matter? But Tito wouldn't hear of it. Yaya would be beside herself, he'd said. And he'd promised her that he would take good care of Carlos. Which meant, they'd be celebrating Christmas with all of their family traditions, just the way they usually did.

"One day, you'll have a family of your own to pass our traditions down to," said Tito suddenly, as though reading his thoughts. "I hope I'm still alive to see it."

"Tito, don't talk like that. Of course you'll be alive to see it."

"I don't know. You haven't had a girlfriend in two years."

Carlos rolled his eyes as he reached for an ornament from the box by his feet marked "Holiday decorations". Carlos had ended the previous relationship when he realised his girl-friend wasn't on the same wavelength as he was about their future. And he'd never felt that connection, the chemistry, that he was hoping to find when he was with her. But Tito couldn't let it go.

"I want great grandchildren before I die. I don't think that's too much to ask. To see you happy, that's my goal. After that, I can leave anytime."

Carlos hated it when Tito talked that way. As though his only purpose in living was to see Carlos have a family. What if it never happened? Carlos wasn't certain he'd ever find someone to share his life with. So far, he'd had no luck in that department. Every woman he dated seemed to have a completely different worldview to him. And it made sense — his life had begun with his pregnant mother running from a drug cartel to a country on the other side of the world. He'd been raised in a family where secrecy was the only way they could keep their relatives back home safe. If the cartel discovered where they were, people they loved could die. So they kept to themselves and stayed away from anyone who might betray them. They'd lived like fugitives. So, it made sense that he found it hard to connect with women who'd never experienced anything like what he had.

"I hear you, Tito," he said. "I know that's what you want. But I can't make it happen. You'll just have to wait."

"I only want you to be happy. I hate to see you so lonely."

"I'm not lonely. I have you." Carlos tried to smile at Tito as the words left his mouth, but they sounded hollow even to him, and his smile was forced. As much as he wanted to reassure his grandfather, he worried how his life would be once Tito was gone. He'd be completely alone. And the thought saddened him. He couldn't tell his grandfather how he felt though, since there wasn't anything either of them could do about it. And besides, it was Christmas — they should be laughing and enjoying their time together.

"Do you remember the Christmas Yaya got that rash all over her face?" asked Carlos, adding another ornament to the tree.

Tito grunted as he rose from his chair to help with the decorating. "Of course. She looked like a big red ornament." He chuckled. "Turned out she was using a new face cream to try to look younger."

"I had to go to the shops and buy her an antihistamine before the swelling would go down," added Carlos.

"Ah, she was always a beautiful woman," mused Tito, bending over to attach an ornament to a branch. He straightened his back. "Even with the red face."

They both laughed together over the memory.

"You know, your mother loved this time of year."

"Oh yeah?" Carlos wished he could remember. He had only a few vague images in his mind of the mother who'd died when he was so young. She was lovely, he remembered that. With long, brown hair and a smile that lit him up on the inside.

"Yes, she loved to sing. Had the most wonderful voice. She'd sing all the carols to you in Spanish, and the two of you would rock in that old hammock we had. Do you remember that? She'd rock you and sing carols until the sun went down, and you'd sit out there together to look at the stars."

Carlos smiled as his grandfather described the scene. He could almost picture it in his mind, although there were only snippets in his memory. "Vaguely. I loved it when we'd sit outside together like that. Most of the time, she was working and so busy. But when we had a chance to spend time together, she gave me all of herself. It was just the two of us, the rest of the world didn't matter when we had each other."

Tito nodded, a smile warming his lips. "Yes, she was a good mother. And a good daughter to me and your Yaya."

"I wish I could remember more about her. It was so long ago."

"I know, *nieto*."

They continued in silence for a few more minutes. Carlos' thoughts turned to Adele, the blonde woman he'd first met when interviewing for the part-time job. She'd struck him as someone he'd like to get to know better. Seeing her fall in the mud at the tree farm had taken away his shyness as he'd been more concerned about helping her than worrying about his own insecurities. The mud on the end of her nose made him want to wipe it away and kiss the tip. Of course, thinking that way was pointless. A woman like her wouldn't be interested in someone like him. No doubt she was already dating a surfer with big muscles and a fancy car. Although if she was, where was he when she was dragging an enormous Christmas tree through the muck on her own? He hoped he'd get a chance to see her again — maybe even work up the courage to ask her out on a date. It'd been so long since he'd done that, he'd almost forgotten how.

"I remember one time, your mother couldn't afford to get you what you wanted for Christmas. You wanted this action figure, I can't remember exactly what it was called. But she was determined to get it for you. I told her, you shouldn't spoil the child, he doesn't need it. But she wouldn't listen to me. She went down to the shops and begged them for a job. They gave her one, stacking shelves. She went every night after work to stack shelves so she could afford to buy that toy for you." His grandfather chuckled. "And she did it. She was a strong woman. Once she set her mind to something, there was no stopping her."

Carlos smiled. "That's right. It was the Jet Blaster Soldier. I wanted it so badly. All the other boys at school had one or were getting one for Christmas. And I knew we couldn't afford it, but I wanted it anyway. I didn't know she'd worked so hard to get it for me though." He pondered his grandfather's words as they decorated the tree. His mother had hidden her struggle from him, or maybe he'd simply overlooked it as most young children did. The knowledge that she'd done that for him, to make him happy, filled his heart with a deep longing to know her and a sadness that he never would.

CHAPTER 6

CINDY

*T*he saucepan bubbled on the stove, and Cindy Flannigan stirred it slowly then took it off the heat. She lifted the wooden spoon to her lips and tasted the eggnog mixture carefully. It was hot but cooled quickly and it tasted delicious. She went back to stirring. It would be ready soon, and it was just as good as it always was. The family looked forward to her eggnog each year. They could drink it cold over ice or add a little rum. It was up to the individual how they took their drink. She preferred it over ice with an extra dash of cinnamon. Even though she'd be away for the holidays, at least the kids would have her eggnog to remind them of her.

There was a knock at the door. She wiped her hands on her apron and hurried to answer it. Diana stood on the front stoop, her brown bob perfectly coiffed, wearing a red polka dot dress and oversized sunglasses. She pulled the sunglasses down her nose.

"Good afternoon, stranger."

Cindy grinned. "Come on in. I'm sorry I haven't seen much of you lately."

"I'm only your best friend. Never mind, I suppose. You're married again, and no longer my neighbour, so I'll have to beg for attention."

"Stop it. You know you mean the world to me," said Cindy, laughing.

Diana followed Cindy into the house, shutting the door behind her. Her eyes twinkled and she leaned in to kiss Cindy's cheek.

"I'm only teasing. But really, you have been terribly neglectful lately."

"Between the wedding, honeymoon, training Adele on how to run the café, and planning this trip to New Zealand, I've been run off my feet. Cup of eggnog, or tea?"

"Tea would be lovely, thank you."

In the kitchen, Diana sank into a chair at the small round table with a sigh. "It's good to get off my feet. I've been walking a lot more. Trying to keep up with exercise now that I'm not running an inn and on my feet all day long."

"That's a good idea. I know what you mean. I feel almost itchy without eight hours a day at the cafe. I've been walking on the beach every morning with Athol."

"Where is Athol?" asked Diana as Cindy set the kettle to boil.

"He's visiting his son in Brisbane before Christmas, since we're going to be away over the holidays. I wanted to go with him, but it was a last-minute trip and I've got to pack. Besides, I'm worried about Adele managing the cafe without me. It gets so busy this time of year, so I've been dropping by each day just to check on her."

Diana shook her head. "Oh dear, I'm sure she loves that."

"She's fine with it."

"Honey, you have to let her stand on her own two feet. You've trained her, shown her the ropes, and now it's time to take a step back and leave her alone."

"But what if…?"

"She'll make mistakes, just like we did when we were starting out. But if she needs your help, she'll give you a call."

Cindy wasn't sure she could do that. Leaving Adele to fail was something she'd always struggled with. It was why she'd been so anxious about Adele living in Darwin. It was too far away, and she couldn't help if something went wrong. But she knew Diana was right. Adele was a grown woman; she'd have to manage on her own someday. Perhaps it was time for Cindy to let her work things out herself, no matter how hard it was.

She filled the teapot with leaves then poured steaming water over them. She carried the pot to the table and found two mugs as well as a jar of freshly made jam drops. She set the jam drops between them and passed Diana a plate and napkin. Then she slipped into the chair opposite her friend.

"You're right. I have to let her live her own life. But it's so hard."

"I know it is. I didn't get to raise Ben myself but having him living so far away with his new wife is harder on me than I thought it'd be. Especially now Rupert is gone. I wish Ben could've lived here in the Cove for longer. Although I'm glad to know he and Vicky are happy in Melbourne."

"Have you heard from them lately?" asked Cindy, taking a bite out of a jam drop.

"Yes, they'll be in Brisbane for Christmas with his parents. They've invited me to come for Boxing Day since I'll be in the Cove for Christmas Day, so I'll be heading up there after breakfast."

"Oh that's lovely," replied Cindy. "I'm so happy for you, Di. Although, I can't believe you're staying on your own in the Cove for Christmas. Athol and I will be in New Zealand, Emily and Ethan are going to Tasmania. You'll be all alone. Wouldn't you rather be with Ben and his family?"

Diana sighed. She set down her tea cup on a side table. "I thought about that a lot. But with Emily and Ethan away for Christmas, I offered to help out at the Manor. They have staff to manage the place, but Emily feels much better about it all with me overseeing things. It's booked solid, so it'll be busy enough to need all hands on deck. And to be completely honest, last Christmas was so hard. It was the first Christmas since selling the bed and breakfast and I'd only recently lost Rupert. It was all a blur. Now that Rupert's gone, I want to spend this Christmas in our old rooms. I'll help manage the breakfast service, but after that I'm going to sit on our former porch and look out over our garden and reminisce a while. I miss it there. I miss him." Her eyes gleamed with unshed tears. "It's how we used to spend the morning after breakfast, and I feel as though I need to honour him that way. I'll probably take a walk in the afternoon or something. But the mornings were our special time together. Besides, I want to give Ben and Vicky space to be with his parents. Next year, I'll spend the day with them. Anyway, I'll probably pop in to see Sarah and Mick around lunch time. I'll see how I feel."

Cindy squeezed her arm. "That sounds like a good plan. And a lovely way to spend your Christmas."

"Thanks, I'm excited to see Ben and Vicky the next day. I'll miss you of course."

Cindy patted the back of her friend's hand. "And I'll miss you as well. Although, I'm so looking forward to seeing Susan. I haven't been to Christchurch in years. And she can't travel much because of her diabetes. I love spending time with her. It's as if we've never been apart when we finally get the chance to catch up. And phone calls aren't the same as visiting."

"That's true," admitted Diana, taking a sip of tea.

Cindy grimaced as her heart skipped a beat for no reason. A cold sweat broke out across her brow, and she massaged it with the tips of her fingers which were suddenly clammy.

"Are you okay?" asked Diana.

"I don't know, my heart feels funny. It seems to be racing or something." She drew a quick breath as her heart fluttered again.

"Maybe you should lie down for a little while, get some rest. You've probably overdone things a bit."

"You might be right. I haven't felt well lately, but I thought it was lack of sleep. Athol wants me to get a check-up, but I decided to wait until after the holidays. There's too much to do." She took another sip of tea, then blinked as her vision blurred. "Oh dear, I think perhaps I should lie down, like you suggested."

Diana helped her to the couch, and Cindy lay on her back with one hand on her forehead. "I'm a little dizzy, I will admit it."

Diana hovered, worry in her eyes. "Would you like me to call an ambulance?"

"No, I don't want to be a bother."

"It's no bother," continued Diana.

Her heart rate continued to pitter-patter in various patterns, and occasionally thudded in a way that startled her. A fast stretch followed by a drop, as though she'd been given a fright. Then, her head spun, and her vision continued to worsen. Finally, when her breathing became more difficult, and her chest felt as though a band squeezed around it, she admitted she needed help and Diana called the ambulance.

"It's probably nothing," she said, between huffing breaths.

"But just in case, would you mind calling Athol for me? And maybe Sarah as well."

Diana got her a glass of water and made additional phone calls while they waited for the paramedics to arrive. She checked on Cindy every few seconds, in a way that would've been irritating if it wasn't so thoughtful. Cindy could always count on Diana.

"I'm glad you're here with me," she said, reaching for Diana's hand and holding it tight.

"I am too. Don't you worry, everything's going to be perfectly okay." Diana's eyes were dark with worry, but she smiled a wobbly smile that didn't reassure Cindy in the least.

What was happening? Was this how a heart attack felt? She wasn't sure. There didn't seem to be any pain, not that she could tell. She tried to recall all the posters she'd seen about the symptoms of a heart attack and vaguely remembered seeing something about pain. Or maybe it was numbness. She did a mental check of her arms and realised they weren't numb. So maybe it wasn't a heart attack after all. Although the irregular heartbeat was concerning and uncomfortable.

She wished she could simply take a deep breath, sit up, and tell Diana not to worry, that she was fine. But she didn't feel fine, perhaps she was having a stroke, or she could simply be dehydrated. But her thoughts were more abstract than concrete, her mind was muddled and her head light.

It might be only a panic attack, rather than anything more serious. If that was all it was, she'd be ashamed to have worried everyone over nothing. And there wasn't a thing she could do about the fuss being made over her now since Diana had reverted to managerial mode, where she took control of the situation and ordered people about as though she was heading up a military operation. She was on the phone barking orders to Athol right at that moment. Poor

Athol, he was probably worried sick about her and so far away he couldn't do anything to help. She should tell Diana not to worry him, but she couldn't manage to get the words out.

To calm herself, Cindy stared at the wall. There was a watercolour painting of a beach scene, with a small, grey half-circle of seagulls, and white-capped waves rolling along a golden shoreline. Black rocky cliffs fenced one end of the beach, and shadowy footsteps etched a winding path in the sand. It was a beautiful painting. She'd bought it from a local artist years earlier and had always loved it. It'd hung on the living room wall in her former house, and now it was here, in the new home she and Athol shared together. There were so many memories wrapped up in that painting. When she looked at it, they flooded back with a rush. Good memories and bad. Arguments with Andy, children squealing with delight, heartbreak over Andy's affairs, and the warmth of loving embraces. So much of her life lived with the painting as a backdrop. It calmed her thoughts, soothed her soul.

When the paramedics arrived, they rushed in with their medical bag and knelt beside her asking questions and testing her heart rate, her blood pressure, her vision, and more.

"How are you feeling now, Cindy?" asked one of the paramedics, a woman with a pile of red curls on top of her head.

"A little better, I think. But still dizzy and my heart rate feels funny."

"Your blood pressure is high and you're experiencing some tachycardia, so I think it would be a good idea if we take you to the hospital and get you checked out by a doctor. What do you say?"

"I'll defer to your judgement," she replied, breathlessly. She didn't like the idea of spending the rest of the day in the emergency room, but the episode had scared her more than she wanted to admit. She didn't feel like herself.

"Let's go and get you checked out. That way we can make sure you're okay." The woman smiled as she packed everything away into her medical bag.

"All right."

They helped her onto a stretcher and rolled her out of the house and down the driveway to the waiting ambulance.

"I'll follow you to the hospital," called Diana as Cindy waved goodbye.

She couldn't answer. She was exhausted from the strain of it all and still breathless. She blew her friend a kiss instead as an acknowledgement.

Throughout the drive to the hospital, the paramedic who sat in the back with her tried to keep her calm by chatting about the weather, her children, and her plans for Christmas. Gradually she began to feel better. Her vision improved, her heart rate settled, and she felt well enough to sit up.

"I think I'm okay now," she said, shifting in place.

The paramedic pressed a hand gently to her shoulder. "That's good to hear, but I need you to stay where you are. We'll be at the hospital soon, and we'll check you into the emergency department."

With a sigh, she looked at the ceiling overhead and hoped someone would put her egg nog away in the fridge before it was ruined.

* * *

SHE'D ALMOST DRIFTED off to sleep when the door to her room flung open and Athol rushed in. He hesitated when he saw her eyes were shut, she heard him slow and stand by the bed in silence. She opened her eyes and offered him a wry smile.

"Surprise!" she whispered.

He grinned. "You had me worried. Diana was almost hysterical on the phone."

"She's more than a little dramatic at times," agreed Cindy, sitting up in the bed and making herself comfortable against a stack of white pillows.

"Have they told you what's going on yet?" he asked.

She shook her head. "They've run every test imaginable. But now I'm waiting for the results to come back. I thought I'd have a little nap. I'm sure it's nothing more than a bit of fatigue."

He pulled a chair up to the bed and sat beside her, holding her hand in his. "We'll find out soon enough. I'm sorry I wasn't here with you. I drove down from Brisbane as soon as I could after Diana called."

She smiled and squeezed his hand. "I'm glad you're here. I've missed you. Did you have a nice time?"

"I did, it was great to see everyone. I only wished you were there too."

"Next time," she replied.

A doctor walked into the room, sporting a white coat and a stethoscope around his neck. He sported a black beard and had a cheerful smile beneath his moustache.

"How are you feeling, Mrs Miller?" he asked.

"Much better, thank you."

"That's wonderful. I'm Dr Anand, and I've got your test results here. It seems you have high blood pressure and high cholesterol."

"Really?" Cindy frowned. She was always careful about her diet and exercised regularly. She'd never had high readings for blood pressure or cholesterol before. "Can they cause the symptoms I experienced?"

He nodded as he flicked through the chart he'd taken from the end of her bed. "That's right. I'm afraid your blood pressure is at a concerning level, so I'm going to put you on some medication to get those numbers back to a place I'm more comfortable with. Then, we can cut back on sweets and fats to try to get your cholesterol under control. I'm going to prescribe something for that as well. More of a temporary fix, I hope. Since I'm sure we'll be able to control your readings with a few dietary changes. Okay?"

"Thank you, Dr Anand."

"I'd like to do some more tests, and I'll be referring you to a cardiologist, to make sure there's nothing wrong with your heart. Although it's not unusual for women your age to have some tachycardia now and then."

"Okay." Women her age. When had she stumbled into that category? It'd happened suddenly, without her permission. Age had a way of doing that which she found most odious. She didn't feel old. Well, most of the time she didn't, anyway. Today was certainly an exception.

The doctor asked various questions, wrote out some prescriptions, then left them alone in the room. Athol cupped her cheek with one hand and kissed her on the lips, gently and lovingly.

"I suppose we should be grateful."

Her brow furrowed. "Grateful?"

"It could've been a lot worse. Blood pressure and cholesterol we can do something about. It's not so bad."

"You're right. Although I still feel pretty awful."

"I'm sure you do. But we'll get the medication and make some lifestyle changes. It'll be fine. And I can help you along the way."

She stroked his cheek, and tears filled the corners of her eyes. "I'm so grateful for you. You always know what to say to help calm me down."

"There is one thing I think we should talk about, though."

"What's that?" she asked.

"I don't know if a flight overseas is a good idea right now. I think we should talk about New Zealand."

Cindy's eyes widened. "Oh no! I can't leave Susan in the lurch this late. She's expecting us for Christmas. And it's been so long since we've seen each other."

"I know, and I'm not saying you shouldn't go. But let's talk about it when you're feeling a little better. Okay?"

Cindy let her eyes drift shut as anxiety washed over her. She couldn't imagine cancelling the trip this late. And now she'd miss out on seeing her sister, as well as putting everyone out. Surely, she would be able to stick to her plans. She could take the medication with her, and everything would be fine.

The door pushed open again and Adele rushed in, her hair pulled into a loose ponytail and an apron still tied around her waist.

"Mum," she exclaimed, hurrying to embrace Cindy. "You're okay."

"Of course, I am," objected Cindy with a frown. "What on earth did Diana tell you?"

"She said she thought you were having a heart attack." Adele kissed Cindy's cheek, then slumped into the chair by the bed, puffing lightly. "Did you?"

"I most certainly did not," replied Cindy with a snort. "Diana Jones is going to get an earful when I see her next."

Adele laughed. "Don't be too hard on her mum. She loves you, that's all. I'm so glad you're okay though."

"I'm fine. And I'm excited for the holidays." She glanced at Athol. "Because there's nothing wrong with me that a little medicine can't fix."

He rolled his eyes. "Yes, dear."

Cindy smiled, but her smile faded as soon as he looked away. She knew he was right, but she didn't want to admit it to him or to herself. What would she tell her sister? They'd planned this trip months ago and had both been so excited about it. Susan had an entire itinerary scheduled for the week they would be in Christchurch. If they didn't go, what would Susan do for the holidays?

With a sigh, she rolled onto her side and stared out the window, listening absently as Adele and Athol discussed her health. She finally had freedom, away from a destructive marriage and the all-consuming cafe that'd dominated every holiday for decades, and now her body had let her down. She worked hard not to cry. It wouldn't be fair to get upset, especially when her health issues weren't as serious as she'd feared only a few hours earlier. But still, it didn't seem fair. Then she almost laughed at her youth-like naiveté and self-pity — she could hear her mother's words, as though the woman stood before her, hands pressed to her ample hips and her brown eyes flashing: *life isn't fair sweetie, the sooner you learn that the better.*

CHAPTER 7

SARAH

The whining and scratching at the back door roused Sarah Flannigan from a light sleep. She rose from the couch and rubbed her eyes. With a quick glance at the bassinet next to her, she confirmed baby Leo was sleeping soundly, with one tiny hand fisted beside his plump, rosy cheek.

She wanted to scoop him up and kiss him, but he'd been crying for hours, and she'd only managed to get him down for a nap less than twenty minutes earlier. So, she resisted the urge and stumbled to the back door to let Oscar inside.

The rescue dog rushed in, tail wagging. Then turned circles around Sarah as she patted his back.

"Thanks for waking me up, buddy. I only got about ten minutes of sleep, but it's so important that you come into the house right now since the sun is going down and your favourite little hole in the garden is in the shade. I get it."

There was no point trying to get back to sleep now since

Leo would wake up hungry before too long. Sarah sat next to a box of decorations and set about pulling them out, untangling them, and working her way around the living room with them. There were strings of beads in gold and red, tinsel, ornaments, even a small church with a working light and a steeple. She loved Christmas. It was her favourite time of year, so she'd built up quite a collection of decorations over the years. Whenever she travelled to a new town or a foreign country, she'd bought a Christmas ornament to hang on her tree. Doing that meant the tree was decorated with an eclectic mix of trinkets that carried cherished memories with them.

She'd been existing in a haze of sleeplessness, feeding, burping, changing, and rocking for the past two months. Soon, it would be Christmas, and she'd had no chance at all to think about it. No shopping done; no meals planned. She didn't even know what the rest of the family would be doing for the holidays. She rarely answered the phone anymore since it inevitably rang when she was in the middle of something with her hands dirty or holding a baby. She felt completely out of the loop, but fine with it at the same time. Sarah loved that most of her day was spent with just her and Leo now that Mick had returned to work. It was a precious — if exhausting — time, and she wouldn't trade a moment of it.

The sound of hammering rang out from the garden shed. Mick must've come home and was working in the shed. He often did that when he had to put together items for clients. He'd come in as soon as it was dark. She hadn't thought about dinner plans yet. She put an ornament on the tree, then padded to the kitchen in bare feet to look through the refrigerator.

There were some lamb chops, along with rosemary and baby potatoes, it would make a delicious and easy meal. She checked for vegetables and found carrots and corn on the cob. That along with some fresh garlic bread would fill the emptiness in her stomach that seemed to be ever present since Leo was born. She couldn't seem to keep the hunger at bay.

A knock on the front door had her immediately on edge, hoping Leo wouldn't wake. She poised on tiptoe, grimacing in silence, but he didn't make a sound. So, she hurried to the front door to keep whoever it was from making any more noise.

"Hi, Mum," she said as the door swung open.

Mum leaned in to kiss her cheek. "Hi, love, I thought you might like some dessert tonight, so I brought you a lemon meringue pie. I would've made it myself, but I've had quite the day. So, I stopped by the cafe and picked one up instead."

"Well, it *is* your recipe," replied Sarah, shutting the door behind them. "Come on in, I was about to get started on dinner. Leo is sleeping which is basically a miracle. But I'll wake him for you if you want a cuddle."

Mum waved a hand. "Oh no, don't do that. I know how hard it is to get them quiet at this time of day. I came to talk to you about something, so I'll sit at the bench while you cook."

Sarah nodded and led the way to the kitchen. "It isn't like you to sit and watch someone else cook, Mum. Are you sure you're feeling okay?"

She helped her mother into a chair at the kitchen table and sat across from her. Mum looked pale, her usually rosy cheeks peaked. Her mother sighed and linked her hands together on the table.

"I went to the emergency room earlier. Diana called you but she said your phone was switched off."

"What?" Sarah covered her mouth with one hand. "What happened?"

"Firstly, I'm fine," replied Mum, reaching for Sarah's hand, and taking it in her own. "I have high blood pressure and cholesterol, plus some tachycardia, but it's really not a big deal. Well, it's nothing that can't be resolved."

"Okay."

"I had some heart palpitations and my vision blurred, but I'm fine. Athol drove me over here, he's on the phone out in the car talking to someone. He'll be in shortly, but I wanted to talk to you alone, first. The doctor gave me some medication that's supposed to help, so I'm sure I'll be back to normal in no time. I'm going to make some changes to my diet and lifestyle as well."

A rush of adrenaline gave Sarah a lightheaded feeling. She couldn't stand the idea of losing her mother. It wasn't something she'd ever thought much about. Mum was healthy and strong, like a rock in her life. She would always be there for her. At least, that was how it'd felt to Sarah until a moment ago.

"Are you sure? Maybe you should rest."

Mum shook her head. "No, I'm fine. I don't want to lie about. You know me. But I'm taking it easy. My only regret is that we won't get to have our Christmas traditions again this year."

"What do you mean?" asked Sarah with a yawn. She rose to her feet to put the kettle on. If she was going to stay awake much longer, she'd need a cup of tea.

"We always spend Christmas in this house but we're going to be away this year. Maybe next year things can go back to normal. Or perhaps I should get used to everything being different now."

Sarah opened a cupboard to retrieve a tea pot and added sweet-smelling tea leaves. "We can have it here. If everyone brings a dish, so I don't have to do all the cooking. And if you don't mind the mess."

"That's a lovely thought," replied Mum. "But I'm not sure there'll be anyone still in the Cove."

"Oh?" Sarah had no idea what her mother was talking about. Her sleep-deprived mind couldn't fix itself on any memory that would explain the direction this conversation was taking.

"I'm going to New Zealand to see Sue. Don't you remember?"

"Oh yeah, that's right. It'd completely slipped my mind." Sarah poured hot water from the jug into the teapot. She yawned again. "I'm sorry, I can't seem to keep track of anything other than Leo these days."

"That's fine, love. You're in the baby haze. That's what I call the first three months. There's very little else that you can focus your thoughts on in those days. It does get better though. And your sister will be in Darwin. Not to mention Ethan and Emily have plans to visit some of her extended family in Tasmania. I'm not sure what your father is doing. But the rest of us will be out of your hair for the holidays."

AFTER HER MOTHER LEFT, Sarah sat sipping the last dregs of tea from her cup and staring out over the darkening garden. Shafts of pink and orange streaked across the deep blue sky. A kookaburra laughed in the distance, soon joined by a chorus of its mates.

Her spirits deflated.

It didn't make sense for her to be upset that the entire family was busy for Christmas. She had a newborn, and her husband, and that was all she'd need to be fulfilled. In spite of that, a twinge of emotion over the fact that they'd all made other plans without consulting her or considering that she might want them around for Leo's first Christmas, flashed

over her. She'd had an idea in her head of how it might go —
aunts, uncles, and grandparents all doting over him, giving
him gifts he couldn't open or appreciate, while she sipped
her mother's famous eggnog in the background with a smile
of maternal pride.

But now it wouldn't happen. And she was disappointed.
The idea of her father and his girlfriend being their only
guests made it worse. She loved Dad, but Keisha was a
handful at the best of times. She complained about everything, judged everyone, and looked down her nose at Sarah
for not slathering her face in makeup or wearing six-inch
stiletto heels every day. Sarah wasn't sure she'd have the
patience for the two of them that she usually would if left
alone with them in her current state.

Leo stirred and began to cry. She lifted him from the
bassinet and wrapped him more tightly in his wrap. He
settled against her chest, and she carried him out the back
door and through the garden to the shed. She found Mick
there, packing away his tools in the gloaming. He wore a
white singlet top and a pair of board shorts. His tanned and
muscular arms glistened with sweat, his blonde hair stood on
end as though he'd run his fingers through it one too many
times.

"Hi, honey," she said, giving him a kiss.

He grinned, the corners of his green eyes crinkling as he
kissed her back, then peeked at Leo through the wrap. "Hey,
and hello to you too little buddy."

"Finished work for the day?" she asked.

He nodded as he shut the shed door and padlocked it.
"Yep, all done. I'm ready for a shower and a sit down." Then
he put his arm around her shoulders, and they walked back
to the house together.

"Mum told me no one from the family will be around for
Christmas. She's going to New Zealand, Adele will be in

Darwin, and Ethan and Emily are headed to Tasmania. I haven't spoken to Dad yet, but it looks like it might just be you, me and Leo for the holidays this year." She did her best to smile around the words, but only managed a brief kind of grimace.

Mick stopped her and cupped her cheeks with both hands. He looked deep into her eyes and kissed her on the lips, with Leo between them.

"That sounds perfect to me."

"Really?" she asked.

"What could be better? The three of us, no stressing or worrying about family drama or cooking for everyone. There's no one else I'd rather spend the day with than the two of you."

"What about your parents?"

"They're in Fiji this year." He shrugged. "They're not big into family gatherings. Much more important to get a good tan."

She laughed. "I'm sorry, honey."

"Don't be," he replied. "It suits me fine. That way I get you and Leo all to myself."

CHAPTER 8

ADELE

22ND DECEMBER

*E*merald Cove revelled in its complete quaint glory at Christmastime. It was the time of year all the local businesses pulled out twinkle lights, tinsel, and fake snow and turned the little hamlet into a sweltering winter wonderland and sang about open fires, dashing through the snow, and white Christmases while the sun beat down on the heads of Cove residents and left their skin reddened, freckled and sore.

The only thing white about Christmas in the Cove were the caps that frothed atop the waves curling to shore on the golden arcs of sand that ran along the entire length of the village.

Adele pushed the pedals on her bike as sweat trickled

down her spine. She puffed into the hot wind, enjoying the feel of it on her skin even if it stifled her a little at the same time. Green wreaths dotted with red poinsettias hung on each lamp post at the roundabout in the centre of town.

As she passed the gelato place, Christmas carols rolled out to greet her, then were gone again, lost in the noise of traffic and the crashing of waves. Her new flat was so close to work, she loved that she could ride her bike to the cafe. It meant she got some exercise and could leave her car at home. Even if she did arrive drenched in sweat, she'd taken to packing a backpack with a change of clothes and a towel so she could have a dip in the ocean and cool off before she had to get started planning out the day, refereeing the staff and ordering supplies.

She pulled the bike onto the footpath by the cafe. It sat closed, still, and silent, with steel bars blocking the usually open doorway. As soon as the padlock snapped open, she pushed her bike inside and shut it again. Then she tucked the key into her backpack and padded down the winding, narrow path that'd been worn into the grass beneath a grove of pandanus trees, to the dunes.

With her backpack tucked into the base of one of the trees, she stripped down to her bright blue bikini and ran down the beach to the waves. With a few leaps she was past the breakers and into the deep, cool ocean. The cold of it snatched the breath from her lungs for a moment, then soothed her body. She ducked beneath a wave, letting the water take the heat from her scalp and hair as well. Within moments the sweat was washed from her body and the relief of the cold water had chased away the stifling heat, leaving her invigorated.

Back at the cafe, she showered and dressed in a floral cotton strappy dress with natural leather sandals. Then she pulled her still-damp hair up into a messy bun. It would dry into tumbling curls giving her the beachy, sun-kissed look that she'd inherited from her mother. She loved that they shared the same blonde hair and blue eyes. They were the only two in the family who had them. Her elder sister Sarah had brown eyes and straight brown hair, and Ethan looked more like their father, with light brown hair. It was something special she shared with her mother, a connection she'd never fully appreciated until recent years when she'd lived so far away and missed Mum more than she'd ever imagined she would.

She glanced at her newly repaired phone screen as she emerged from her office into the kitchen. She was checking to see if Antoine had called, but of course he hadn't. She'd blocked his number. He hadn't tried to contact her in any other way since their last conversation either. Maybe he finally understood that it was over and there was nothing he could say to change that. She tried to measure how she felt about that, and realised she was good with it. Happy in fact.

While she was dressing, a few of the staff had arrived to get ready for the breakfast rush. The cafe would open in an hour and the cook, Francesca, was already slicing, dicing, and prepping everything needed for meal service. One of the wait staff, Brooke, sat on the bench, her legs swinging as she munched on a banana.

Francesca sighed, as she sliced bacon into strips. "Get off my counter."

"What?" asked Brooke, still munching and swinging. Her black converse shoes contrasted perfectly with her pink shorts and white T-shirt. She wore a pink sweat band around her head and her long, bleached-blonde hair hung down her back in a thin ponytail.

"I don't want you sitting there. I've already wiped it

down. Everything in my kitchen is clean, and here you come along and mess it up with your big old butt on my shiny counter."

Brooke's brow furrowed and she slipped from the bench, landing with a plop on her feet on the tiled floor. "Don't have to be mean about it."

"Yes, I do. I've told you the same thing about a million times. Does nothing get through that skull of yours?" Francesca set down her knife and pressed her gloved hands to her apron-covered hips, her face like thunder. "Your generation. Pfffft." She threw her hands up in the air and rolled her eyes. "You think the world is yours and everything in it." Then she returned to her slicing.

Adele hovered in the background. She wasn't sure what to do about the bickering between staff members that seemed to have increased in recent weeks. She was the newest member of staff and almost the youngest. It was hard for her to step in and break up the back and forth that was almost a daily occurrence, but it didn't sit right with her. She didn't want to be the kind of boss that cracked down on her staff, who couldn't let them speak up. But she had a sense that if she didn't do something about it, it could cause issues for the entire business.

"Um, Brooke, can I see you in my office please?"

Brooke followed her into the office and slumped into a chair. Adele closed the blinds and sat at her desk, facing the waitress.

They exchanged pleasantries for a few minutes and Adele swallowed hard before broaching the subject she'd called her in for. "I can't help noticing some tension has developed between you and Francesca."

Brooke shrugged and examined her cuticles.

Adele cleared her throat. "Well, is there anything you want to talk about?"

"Not really. It's no biggie."

Adele pressed her lips together as she framed her thoughts into words. This was harder than she'd thought it would be. Her first instinct at any sign of conflict was to keep her head down and leave before she was dragged into it. But as the cafe manager, she had to insert herself directly into the middle of the drama and it made her palms sweat.

"I'd like to see you show Francesca some respect please. She's the head cook here at the cafe, and that makes her a senior staff member. If she asks you to do something, you do it. Do you understand?"

Brooke shifted in her seat, her eyes darkening. "She's a bully."

"No, she's your supervisor. She's in charge. I run the cafe, so she answers to me, but you answer to her. Do you understand?"

Brooke's nostrils flared. "Whatever."

"And that means if she has rules, like no one sits on the counters, then you follow them. She goes to a lot of trouble to keep our food top quality and the kitchen hygienic, wearing hair nets and chef's caps, gloves, and washing and cleaning everything frequently. She doesn't want you to come in and ruin that. Neither do I. Our priority is to our customers, and they expect and deserve a high-quality meal which doesn't include your hair or some grime from your jeans in it. Okay?"

Brooke nodded. "Fine."

"Thank you, Brooke."

The girl hustled from the room in a huff, slamming the door shut behind her. Next, Adele spoke to Francesca and filled her in on the newly minted policy, decided on by Adele five minutes earlier, that there be no attitude, snarky comments, words in anger, or anything remotely resembling those things among the staff. And she asked the cook to help her to monitor that to build a better team environment. When Francesca left the office, Adele crumpled over her desk and lay with her palms and cheek pressed to its cool timber surface for a full minute before moving.

When her mobile rang, she answered with eyes still shut. "Hello?"

"Hi, honey," said Mum. "Calling to see if you need me to pop down to the cafe today. I'm trying to rest, but I could probably make it if you want me to."

Adele straightened in her chair and opened her eyes. "No Mum, I don't need you here. Are you feeling any better?"

"Much better today, actually. Almost back to normal, I think. Although, my head is still a little light."

"What did the doctor say about traveling?"

"Oh, he doesn't think I should go. But I can't back out now. Sue is expecting me." Mum groaned. "It's unfair, and I know that makes me sound like a whiny baby, but I can't help it. That's how I feel."

Adele agreed with the sentiment. Her mother had worked so hard for so long, raising children, growing the cafe business. She rarely took holidays, hadn't done nearly as much travel as she'd dreamed of doing over the years. And now, when she finally had the time, her health had let her down.

"I'm sorry, Mum. And I don't think you're being a baby about it. It's so frustrating for you. But I think you should listen to your doctor. Anyway, you can visit her later. Right?"

"Hmmm. I suppose so. I'll think about it. Athol says the same thing, we can visit Sue and Bart when the medication has my blood pressure and cholesterol under control. But at this stage, the trip is still on."

"I know you're upset, Mum. That's normal. But you should probably take a deep breath and accept it — that's what you always tell me. Accept the things you can't change."

Mum sighed. "You were listening, huh?"

"I was." Adele laughed.

"Well, I'll think about it. But I'm determined to go if I feel up to it. Did you remember to get the supplies order in yet?" Mum changed tack without warning, catching Adele by surprise. She had a habit of doing it, yet it never failed to throw her, especially when Mum was pointing out something that Adele should've remembered but hadn't.

Adele slapped her forehead with one palm. "No, not yet."

"I think I should come down there…"

"No, I'm fine. I'll put the order in now. It's not too late. I've been busy, that's all. I had to talk to Francesca and Brooke about their bickering."

"Oh?" Mum didn't say more, but she left space in the conversation for Adele to continue. She knew how much her mother was dying to ask questions but didn't want to overstep. She'd been a wonderful support for Adele at the café, and Adele didn't hesitate to ask her advice or for help whenever she needed it. But she didn't want to draw her mother back into the dramas at the cafe. Still, she couldn't help sharing a little bit about what was going on, since her mother was clearly interested, and she could do with some sound advice. The worst thing about being the boss was having no one to turn to when things got hard.

"They were fighting again, and I don't like the way it makes the entire group feel. I want us all to get along, to be a team. And it's getting worse all the time. It's not only them, everyone's been arguing and criticising one another. I've had enough of it, honestly."

"What are you going to do about it?" asked Mum.

Adele chewed on a fingernail. It felt impossible. What could she do about it? She was only one person. One young, small, afraid-of-conflict person. What she really wanted, no needed, was for someone to tell her what to do about it. But that was the problem — she was in charge, it was up to her.

"I don't know. I spoke to the two of them, but I'm afraid it won't make any difference."

"It will, honey. That's a good first step. But I think perhaps you need to have a staff meeting, get everyone in a room and lay out your expectations. You have to nip this stuff in the bud before it becomes a workplace culture. Trust me, I've been there, done that. You don't want it getting out of hand."

* * *

BY THE TIME Adele finished her conversation with her mother and got the supplies order submitted, she was ready to get out of her office. She liked to do a walk around the cafe sometime during breakfast to check on how well it was operating. Everyone had left her alone so far, which was a good sign. If there was anything wrong, they'd have knocked on her door before now.

She strode through the kitchen and out to the cafe, anxious about running into Brooke or Francesca again. If they were still bickering, what would she do about it? She didn't know. But she couldn't stay hidden away in her office all day. With only three days until Christmas, the place was full. Every table held at least one customer, most had three or four. People were talking, laughing, eating, and sipping coffee. The restaurant smelled like coffee, bacon and cinnamon from the bacon and egg wrap special, and the Christmas cappuccinos that brought in guests from all over the coast this time of year.

For the next half an hour, Adele hurried to help the wait staff by bussing tables, or refilling water glasses. She chatted with the regulars and helped tourists locate the best swimming beaches, or the nearest leisurewear boutiques. Then, she spotted Samuel. His white hair stood on end, partially combed over a bald pate. His small, black and white dog sat on a chair beside him eating tidbits from Samuel's fingers. He seemed to be talking to the dog all the while. The animal cocked its head to one side as though pondering something his owner had said.

"Good morning, Samuel," she said, coming up alongside him.

He grinned and pushed his glasses back up his nose. "Hello, Adele. How lovely to see you again."

"How is your breakfast today?"

"I had the waffles with syrup and berries, and it was delicious. Even Eddy agrees. And he's a picky eater."

She laughed. "That's good to hear. Can I get you anything else?"

He shrugged. "Another cup of coffee would be lovely, although I really shouldn't."

"You only live once," she replied with a wink. "I'll get that for you and be right back."

She was about to walk away when she spied the spine of a book poking up from beneath a folded newspaper on the edge of his table. *The Lost Things* was her favourite book of all time, although this copy had the title in English and Spanish. And there it was, half hidden away and dog-eared, like her own copy. "I love that book."

He followed the direction her finger was pointed.

"Oh yes, I do too. It was written by a Colombian. Did you know that?"

"Really? I didn't realise. How wonderful. It's my favourite. The prose is amazing, and the descriptions…"

"It's like you're really there," he completed her thought for her.

"Yes, exactly." She smiled. "Do you enjoy reading?"

"It's the best pastime for someone my age. That and fishing. I can't climb mountains anymore, you see."

"You were a mountain climber?" Her eyes widened. It was something she'd always wished she was brave enough to try. But flying over mountains was as close as she'd gotten to doing it. Unless you counted the mountains in southern Queensland, which weren't nearly as high as those in other parts of the world.

"It was something I enjoyed in my younger years. But no more." He patted his rotund belly. "I got too lazy."

She grinned. "Well, it's amazing you ever did it if you ask me."

"I like cake far too much to keep it up, anyway."

"You do? I have an amazing hummingbird cake recipe that I've been meaning to tweak for the cafe menu. I have to try it out a few times to get it just right before we add it. I was planning to spend the afternoon doing just that. How about I bring you one? I guarantee you'll love it if I don't mess it up too much." She laughed, tucking a strand of hair behind her ears.

He stood to his feet and took her hand in his, cupping it between them both and squeezing. "That is too much. I don't want you to go to so much trouble. You're young, you should be out having fun with other people your own age."

She huffed out a breath of air. "I don't know many people my age. And it's no trouble at all. I've got to cook them anyway, and I'd hate for them to go to waste."

"You know," he began, his smile widening. "I have a grandson who loves cake as much as I do. He's visiting me later. You should meet him. I think the two of you would really get along."

As she walked away, she smiled to herself, imagining the look on Samuel's face when she brought him the cake. There was something special about baking for people. She'd done it for as long as she could remember. She loved bringing joy to people that way. It was why working at the cafe was so rewarding for her — it was a way to connect with people, to give them a little happiness in their day. It fulfilled her in a way that flying never had.

CHAPTER 9

CARLOS

*T*he retirement community was peaceful. A seagull glided on a warm breeze nearby, the occasional call the only thing that broke the stillness of the morning. In the distance, the constant soft roar of the ocean was a like a balm to his soul. The stress and tension he'd felt a few hours earlier had dissipated. Although, thinking about everything he had going on made his shoulders tighten and brought a stabbing pain in one temple. He was still looking for work, his rent would be due on the first of the month, the summer class he was taking to catch up on what he'd missed while moving his grandfather to Emerald Cove involved reading a billion pages of a dry and uninspiring treatise on statistical research methods during which he fell to sleep every ten minutes. This combination of factors wreaked havoc on his nerves. All he wanted to do was find a job that would pay his bills and get him through his PhD so he could finally be a psychologist.

It was what he'd wanted for as long as he could remember — to help people. He loved listening. Listening to stories, to the things that people weren't saying that he could read in their body language. He wanted to be part of the solution, to bring healing to people's minds so they could be the best versions of themselves in their lives. But getting there had taken him seven years so far, and he still had three to go. It was a mammoth effort, and meanwhile, he continued working minimum wage jobs at the age of twenty-five, while he studied every chance he got. Not to mention taking care of his sometimes stubborn, always feisty grandfather. It was a lot. And he often wished his mother or grandmother were still around to help.

He tugged a spindly weed from the garden bed, then reached for another one, his bare hands smarting from the prickly stem. His grandfather had gardening gloves some-where, but they still hadn't unpacked every box after the move. They should've by now, there was really no excuse, except that neither one of them was particularly domestic. And they made do with whatever they had, most days. With Carlos living elsewhere and occupied with his studies and job hunting, Tito was mostly on his own.

They'd lived together in Sydney. But when Tito decided to move, he said he wanted his own place, and that was that. Carlos knew it was really because he thought his grandson should have a life and he didn't want to get in the way of that. He'd admitted as much a few times when they'd argued about where he should live. But Carlos didn't see it that way. They were family, and family stuck together. Still, Tito wouldn't budge when it came to his living arrangement. And so, they lived ten minutes apart and Carlos still spent most of his spare time at Tito's anyway.

He pulled another weed, then another from the firm, dry

soil, then sat for a minute on his haunches, enjoying the sun on his face and the taste of salt in the air.

A bicycle made its way up the street. It climbed the slope at a steady pace. There was a basket on the front of the bike, with something balanced in it. A woman stood on the pedals, in a pair of bright yellow shorts and sporting a white helmet. She pedalled hard, the nose of the bike weaving with the effort. He watched a moment, then returned to his weeding. The garden bed out the front of Tito's small unit was wild and unkempt. The previous owner had left it neglected for years. Tito loved a pretty garden with colourful flowers. It was one of the few things Carlos could do to make the place more homely for his grandfather, so he'd decided to make it a priority.

He was still working when the woman pulled the bike to a stop and hauled it up over the curb. He glanced up to see the woman from the Christmas tree lot, Adele, standing in front of him. She held the bike by its seat, shielding her eyes from the sun with her free hand.

"Carlos, how lovely to see you again."

He stood to his feet, straightened the kinks from his back, and dusted the dirt from his hands. "Hi."

He couldn't say more. His mind raced to understand what she was doing in Tito's front yard. She stared at him a few moments longer, a wide smile on her pretty face. Her blonde hair blazed golden in the glaring sunlight where it poked out beneath the helmet.

He blinked. "Can I help you?"

She laughed. "I came to see Samuel. Does he live here?"

"My grandfather? I didn't realise you two knew each other."

She squinted. "He's your…?"

"Yep."

"Oh. Well, isn't that a coincidence?" Her smile widened. "I

brought him a cake." She pointed to the basket on the front of her green bicycle. A Tupperware container perched there. Her face was red from the heat, sweat trickled down the sides of her face. She wore a pair of bike shorts and a crop top in fluorescent yellow.

"How kind," he replied. "Come inside, I'll find him for you. I'm sure he's fallen asleep in front of the telly. There's a soccer match on and it's difficult to pull him away."

He opened the front door and held it for her then followed her inside. He showed her to a seat in the kitchen at the small round table where they ate their meals together. Then, he rushed to check the cozy lounge, then the bedroom. Tito sat on the bed, propped up against a mound of pillows. A television set on the wall played a soccer game with the sound on mute. Tito's eyes were shut and he snored softly.

Carlos shook his shoulder gently. "Tito, wake up. You have a visitor."

Tito snorted once, as his eyes blinked open. "What? Huh?"

"Adele is here. She brought you a cake."

Tito wiped the corner of his mouth with his sleeve, then smiled. "Adele is here? What a sweet girl she is. Pretty too." He winked at Carlos, who shook his head.

"Yes, very pretty. Come on, she's waiting in the kitchen."

"THE AIM OF GAME, is not to let the ball touch the ground." Tito tapped the small, cloth ball with the side of his foot, sending it into the air. It bounced off his toe, then his other foot. His eyes gleamed.

Carlos watched him, a smile on his face. He'd seen Tito play Fuchi a thousand times. No one was better. Even though he'd slowed down in recent years, he always managed to keep the ball off the ground for longer than Carlos could.

"Wow, that's amazing," said Adele, her brow furrowed. "How do you do that?"

"Practice," replied Tito, still tapping the ball into the air with a toe or the side of his foot. "That is why Carlos cannot beat me. He doesn't put in the time it takes to practice."

Carlos laughed. "I have other things to do with my time, Tito."

Tito winked. "You see, he has no commitment."

They stood in the small courtyard behind Tito's place. The previous owners had let it become a jungle, but Carlos had managed to tame some of the worst weeds and overgrown plants.

Tito let the ball fall to the ground, then swooped into a mock bow while Adele clapped. Carlos joined in with a shake of his head. Tito had always been a showoff. It was one of the most endearing things about his grandfather, and something he definitely had not inherited. Where Tito was the life of the party, Carlos preferred quiet solitude.

"Time for a cup of coffee," said Tito, sinking into one of the wrought iron chairs that surrounded a small, wrought iron table. On the table sat a pot of coffee, three mugs, and one of the cakes Adele had brought.

She sat across from Tito, with Carlos beside her. He poured the coffee while she sliced the cake.

"So, I need you both to be completely honest with me. I'm trying out hummingbird cake recipes for the cafe menu, and I've brought three along today. We have to try all three of them, and then rank them according to which one is the best — it should be tasty, moist, and sweet, but not too sweet."

"I think I can do that," said Carlos, pushing out his chest.

"I was made for this," added Tito, copying his grandson's movement.

Adele pushed a plate with a small slice of cake in front of each of them with a smile. "Remember, honesty please. I don't mind if you don't like it. It won't hurt my feelings — this is for work."

Both men tried all three cakes, and neither of them could decide between them. Adele tried them as well, and they all ate until they could hold no more. The coffee helped to cut the sweetness for Carlos, who didn't have a big sweet tooth. Although, he had to admit that he liked the cake more than he usually did with baked goods. It wasn't too sweet but had a unique flavour that tickled his tongue.

"I love them all. Not sure I'm the best person for the job, since I can't tell much of a difference between any of them."

"There must be something you can point out," said Adele.

He shrugged. "I guess the third one was a little drier than the other two, and the second one wasn't quite as sweet, which I like."

"So the second cake was your favourite?"

"Yep." He took another bite of it, chewed thoughtfully. "Definitely the second cake."

"I agree," said Tito, finishing off his slice then pushing the plate away with a sigh. "I can't eat another bite."

"Great," replied Adele, making a note in her phone. "The second cake is the winner."

"I love how you do market research," replied Carlos. "Two people polled and you're ready to make a commitment to a particular recipe."

She laughed. "What else do you suggest?"

"No, I think it's great. I'm studying to be a psychologist, and we learn about statistics, and analysing data for patterns. It's so intense. I think I'd rather simply ask two people and find a third as a tie breaker if needs be. It would make things so much simpler."

Tito stood to his feet with a groan and ambled into the house with a wave over his head. "I'm off, got a football match to watch. Thanks for the cake, Adele."

She said goodbye, then began cleaning up the cake and plates.

Carlos stood to his feet and picked up Tito's hacky sack. It was dark blue and old, and the beans inside it had shrunk, or been squashed, so that the cover was a little loose.

He dropped it to one foot, then tapped it into the air, kicking and tapping it back and forth to keep it in the air. Adele returned from the kitchen to get the remaining dirty plates and studied him with a smile.

"Hey, you're pretty good at it too."

He caught the ball and set it on the table. "Why don't you try it?"

Adele eyed the ball. "Okay. Although I can tell you right now, I won't be any good at it. I've never tried."

She flicked the ball towards a foot, and it landed with a splat on the ground. She laughed, picked it up and tried again. This time she managed to keep it in the air for three touches before it fell to the ground.

"See, you're getting better already," he said.

She laughed. "It's fun. But I can't imagine ever being as good as Samuel." She wiped the sweat from her brow with the back of her hand.

The two of them walked into the kitchen with the last of the mugs and plates. The small structure had a cozy kitchen with brown cupboards and white bench tops. There were candles scattered throughout the kitchen and attached living room. Paper lanterns lined the windowsills. Carlos had spoken to Tito about the fire hazard, but Tito wouldn't decorate for Christmas any other way. And Carlos would've been disappointed if he did. He loved the traditions Tito and Yaya had continued and passed down to him over the years. They reminded him of happier times when he was younger, when they'd all celebrated together and remembered his mother.

"So, you live here with your grandfather?" asked Adele, as she washed a dirty plate in the sink.

"No, I have a place in town. But Tito wanted to move here from Sydney. Said his house there was too big for him and held too many memories. He wanted to start over again. And he's always loved the idea of living near the beach but couldn't afford it before now. His house in Sydney sold for enough to cover the cost of this flat, and with some left over for him to live off." Carlos picked up a tea towel to dry the dishes as Adele washed them.

He ached a little at how close she was to him, almost close enough to touch. If only there was something he could do about it. But that wasn't like him. Wasn't his personality at all. He wasn't the kind of man to grab a woman and kiss her, as much as he wished he was. Because no matter what he felt, he didn't know that she reciprocated his feelings. And the idea of her pulling away, horrified eyes bulging and wide, was more than he was willing to risk.

She was nice. Could be a friend, given enough time. And he didn't have a single friend in Emerald Cove yet. He could use one. The last thing he wanted to do was to drive her away with an ill-timed kiss. But the heat from her arm as it grazed his was hard to ignore.

"I was living with Mum until recently but got my own place as well. It's small and kind of old, but I love it." She smiled up at him, shaking the dishwater from her hands.

"What about your dad?"

She shrugged. "He and Mum are divorced. He lives in the Cove too, though. I see him every week, but we're not as close as we used to be."

"I'm sorry," he replied. "It's good you live near each other, though."

"Where are your parents?"

He swallowed. This conversation was always the worst to

have; people didn't know how to respond when he told them about his family history. "They're both dead."

"Oh."

"At least, I think my father's dead. If not, he's living in Colombia, and I never met him. In fact, I don't even know his name. Tito refuses to talk to me about him. My mother was pregnant with me when she, Tito, and Yaya, my grandmother, arrived in Australia. But she died when I was five. Brain aneurism, they said."

Adele pressed a hand to her chest, her eyes glistening. "I'm so sorry. How horrible."

"It's okay. It was a long time ago. I don't remember much about her, so it doesn't really upset me to talk about. Yaya died last year, that was much harder."

"What do you think of the Cove so far?" asked Adele, changing the subject.

He cocked his head to one side. "So far, it seems nice. Everyone's friendly, the weather is always hot, and the ocean is beautiful."

"Yeah, that sums it up pretty well." She laughed. "Have you been out for a surf yet?"

"I don't surf."

"Well, you can't live in Emerald Cove and not learn how to surf. I'll take you out sometime."

He grinned. "I'd love that."

CHAPTER 10

ADELE

"*D*o you think Sarah is coping with the baby?" asked Cindy, as she folded a T-shirt into her open suitcase. "Maybe Athol is right, I shouldn't go to New Zealand, after all."

Adele hesitated as she scanned the shelves in her mother's walk-in closet. "What do you mean? Of course, she's coping. She's Sarah."

"She doesn't always cope, Adele."

Adele walked out of the closet holding a zippered jacket in her arms. "Yes, she does. Everything she tackles, she conquers. Nothing fazes her."

"She's very strong, but she has her moments. Just like the rest of us. And babies are hard. Especially the first one. You don't have any idea what you're doing, your whole life gets turned upside down, you're not sleeping…and next thing you know you've burned dinner and fallen asleep on the kitchen table. Or worse, you're running half-naked through the garden in the middle of the night looking for the baby who is tucked safe and sound in her cot."

Adele lay the jacket on her mother's blue and white bed covers and crossed her arms over her chest. "Are you talking about Sarah, or yourself? And why were you half naked?"

Mum shrugged. "It doesn't matter. What matters is your sister's mental health. I'm worried about her."

"Is there a reason, has she done something?" Adele's long fingers drummed a beat on her arm.

"Nothing especially, but she seems very tired. And when I reminded her I was going away for the holidays, she acted like it was the first time she'd heard the news. I think she even sobbed."

"Sarah sobbed?" Adele arched an eyebrow. She couldn't remember the last time she'd seen her resilient sister cry, let alone sob about something so innocuous. Perhaps Mum had a point.

"Yes. At least, I think she did. Anyway, will you please check on her while I'm gone."

"You forget, Mum. I'm leaving tomorrow as well. We're both going to be out of town."

"Oh yes, that's right." Mum slumped onto the bed and scrubbed her face with both hands. "I don't know why that slipped my mind. I was hoping you'd spend Christmas with Sarah and Mick so you could keep an on eye on them."

"I suppose I could cancel." She'd been thinking about it a lot. Ever since yesterday, when she'd spent time with Carlos and Samuel, she'd pondered the idea of staying home for the holidays instead of going to Darwin. Why would she fly to a city where she might run into her ex and his happily pregnant wife, when she could stay home in the Cove with her family? And if she happened across Carlos while cycling around town, or at the cafe, that would be a nice surprise.

"Would you?" pressed Mum. "That would take a load off my mind."

"Okay, I suppose I can. I'll call and cancel my flight and let Bec know. I'm sure she doesn't care. I was gatecrashing her family Christmas anyway. I didn't want to be here in the Cove alone, and she invited me. So…"

"Alone? You wouldn't be alone."

"You know what I mean. I didn't want to third-wheel it with Sarah and Mick, the happy newlyweds, and their perfect baby."

Mum eyed her through narrowed lids. "That's a bit jaded for a twenty-four-year-old, love."

Adele huffed. "I'm not jaded. Well, not really. But you know what I mean."

"I suppose that makes sense."

"If you want me to stay to help though, I'm happy to do that. In fact, I've been concerned about leaving the cafe so soon after taking over."

"I can understand that," replied Mum with a shake of the head. "I've missed many a trip because of that place."

"But you're not going to miss this one," replied Adele with determination as she reached for another shirt to fold for her mother's suitcase.

"Maybe you should invite someone to come along with you, so you don't feel that way?" suggested Mum, as she searched her white antique dressing table for items of makeup to pack into her makeup bag.

"Maybe."

"Any ideas?"

Adele smiled. "There is a guy."

"Oh, really? Do tell?"

"It's nothing really. But I met this guy, his name's Carlos, and he and his grandfather are new to town. They probably don't have anyone else to share Christmas with. It might be nice to include them in ours."

"I'm sure Sarah and Mick wouldn't mind. You should ask."

Adele nodded as the thought took root in her mind. "Okay, I will."

She didn't really believe in coincidences. Things happened for a reason. So when she'd connected with Samuel, then separately with Carlos, the fact that they were related was a detail she couldn't get past. She'd been thinking it over all day. Carlos was handsome, caring and obviously kind. The way he'd taken care of his grandfather was a good sign as far as she was concerned — he had integrity. It was clear how much the two of them loved one another. And she hated the idea of them spending Christmas alone after experiencing so much grief and loss. The idea of spending Christmas together gave her an extra jolt of holiday spirit.

Her only concern was her judgement. She'd already proven to herself that she wasn't the best judge of character when it came to men. What if Carlos was married, or an axe murderer? There was no way for her to know, and her integrity meter seemed to be completely faulty when it came to attractive men. She should've asked him if he was in a relationship. She hadn't seen a ring on his finger, but then again married men didn't always wear one. Antoine certainly hadn't when she'd fallen in love with him. It wasn't until later that his ring had appeared. He'd pulled it from his locker after a shift and shoved it onto his perfectly tanned ring finger. When she'd stopped short, with shock written across her face, he'd blushed pink and stammered a quick explanation about a wife whom he was separated from but who couldn't seem to let him go. He was wearing the ring, he said, out of compassion for her mental health. He wasn't sure what she might do if she saw him without it, but he'd break it to her gently and soon, that it was over, and he wasn't going back.

Of course he didn't do what he'd promised.

Mum sat still on the bed, listening to the crooning of Harry Connick Junior's Christmas carols over her sound system. Then, she sighed. "I don't know, love. Maybe I shouldn't go away either."

"Why not? Because of your health?" asked Adele. "Because, like you said, you've missed so many trips in the past. You don't want to miss this one as well. Sarah will be fine, I'm taking care of the cafe. You can go and have a good time. Unless you're worried…"

Athol walked into the bedroom, smiling when he saw Adele. "I thought I heard voices. When did you get here?"

"Hi, Athol, I've been here about half an hour. Helping Mum pack for your trip."

He arched an eyebrow. "Oh? Are we still going, then?" He reached for Mum and kissed her on the forehead. "Hello, my darling. How are you feeling?"

Mum nodded. "I'm okay."

"Aren't you well, Mum? I thought the medicine was working." Adele reached out to press a hand to her mother's arm.

"It seems I might be reacting to the medication. I'm feeling nauseated and my head is foggy."

"That's not good," replied Adele, her brow furrowing with concern.

"I'm sure it'll all work out. But I've spent the whole morning trying to decide whether or not we should still take this trip."

"We can go later," called Athol as he walked into the closet. "There's nothing stopping us from visiting in a few weeks when things settle down."

"I know. Oh, Sue will be so disappointed." She shook her head. "I'm so disappointed."

Adele sat beside her mother on the bed and looped an arm around her shoulders. "It's okay, Mum. Auntie Sue will understand. It's more important you take care of your health. And like Athol said, you can visit as soon as you're feeling better."

"I suppose you're right," replied Mum. "Merry Christmas to me."

CHAPTER 11

CINDY

*T*he bubbling aftermath of a wave rushed up the beach. The cool water lapped around Cindy's toes as she and Athol strode along the beach. She tightened her grip on his hand and glanced up at him. His grey hair whipped up high over his head with the wind, giving him a wild windswept look. It suited him, she decided. He was usually so well-groomed, with his hair combed to the side, she liked the unkempt look on him.

"How are you feeling?" asked Athol.

She chewed on her lower lip, considering a response. It was hard to know sometimes if the things she felt were real or if she'd talked herself into believing they were. "I'm okay. My brain is still foggy, and I'm tired. Plus, there's a bit of nausea, which might be from the medication. But it's not too bad."

"I'm sure you'll feel better in a couple of weeks," he replied.

"I wish we were still going on the trip," said Cindy.

Athol smiled at her. "I know. But there'll be other trips."

"I hope so."

"Of course there will. We've only recently retired, plus we're newlyweds. Both of us have a lot of living to do. The grandchildren are starting to arrive. We've got to take advantage of the window of opportunity to do the things we want to do."

He was right, but sometimes it felt as though everything around her conspired to ruin her plans.

"So, in the new year perhaps?"

"Definitely. We can go to New Zealand and then head off for somewhere else after that. What do you think?"

"Well, I've always wanted to tour around the South Island." She'd seen so many friends trundle off to New Zealand and spend weeks touring around the beautiful South Island in RVs, or rental cars. Andy had never wanted to do it. His idea of a holiday was a week in Noosa. He didn't like to go far, and with the cafe to care for she hadn't fought him over it, even with disappointment washing away her joy like a dumping wave.

"That sounds perfect. And maybe we can spend some time in Fiji afterwards. I've always loved it there. It's so relaxing."

She grinned at the thought. "Yes, please."

They walked along quietly for a few minutes, listening to the caw of seagulls and the shushing waves. They were small today, almost trickling to shore. The water heaved and sighed, sparkling azure beneath the hot sun.

"Despite the disappointment, I'm happy to stay home for Christmas," she said suddenly.

He kissed the back of her hand. "Me too. It feels right to be here for Leo's first Christmas. Doesn't it?"

"I was sad at the prospect of missing him open his first

gift. Although, he'll probably only whack it with his little fist, but still," admitted Cindy. "I know it's silly, he won't know anything about it and will probably sleep through most of the day, but it's a special time."

"Not silly at all. Those are the things that matter. In fact, on that note there's something I wanted to talk to you about. You know I visited Marcus and Anna recently."

Marcus was Athol's son, and Anna his wife. Cindy knew Marcus from when he was a little boy, although he'd changed a lot since then. He wasn't the carefree, sweet child with the dark brown bowl-cut she remembered.

"Yes, you said you had a nice time."

"I did, but of course there's still tension there. He blames me for some of his issues from childhood."

"Like what?" asked Cindy, her brow furrowed. "From what I recall, he had a pretty idyllic upbringing."

"That's true, from one perspective," agreed Athol. "You never knew this, but his mother had something of a nervous condition. She was a good mother. But every now and then she'd stay in bed, couldn't seem to pull herself out of it."

"No, I didn't realise that." She squinted against the afternoon sun as it set behind Emerald Cove. Streaks of orange glanced off the roofs of the buildings almost blinding her. She adjusted her sunglasses.

"Yes, well she wanted me to keep it quiet. Was ashamed, you see. Anyway, it had an impact on Marcus, and because she's no longer with us he can't blame her. So, he takes it out on me."

"That makes sense, I suppose. Although it's not right."

"I don't mind. If it helps him."

One of the things that'd always impressed Cindy about Athol, even back when they were friends raising children with their respective spouses, was his ability to put his own feelings aside. If he could help someone, he would. Even if it meant making a sacrifice. It was what set him apart from Andy, who always looked out for himself. Athol had been the contrast that'd highlighted to her all those years ago, just how much Andy fell short of the man she'd hoped he would be. Athol was the man she'd longed for, even if she hadn't realised it at the time. Now she knew it. He was the one for her.

"Is there anything we can do?" she asked.

Athol hesitated, then stopped walking and waited until she stood before him, looking up in expectation into his kind, handsome face.

"He says there is. He and Anna are going through some financial difficulty."

Cindy braced herself. "Oh?"

"He made a bad investment, I'm sure you remember me talking about it last year. Anyway, they lost a significant nest egg on the investment. They'd saved it to put down a deposit on a house they have their hearts set on buying. They want to have a family, it seems."

"That's wonderful, they'll make loving parents. I wish them all the best. But…"

"But?" replied Athol, one eyebrow raised.

Cindy sighed. They'd never argued. She and Athol hadn't had a real disagreement so far in their entire relationship. It'd been pure bliss. But she had a very strong feeling she was about to stoke their first.

"But…I don't think it's wise to give money to family. It only gets in the way and causes conflict."

What she wanted to say was, Athol was too soft-hearted. If Marcus and Anna couldn't manage their finances, bailing them out wouldn't help them learn. They should grow and mature through their mistakes, just like she had done. Most likely Athol had learned the hard way throughout his life as well. Everyone experienced the scuffles and hard knocks of life and learning how to navigate those hard times was what built character for the years ahead.

Athol didn't reply. He dropped Cindy's hand as they strode along the beach. She trotted beside him, barely keeping up.

"I know you love him and want to help. We all do as parents. It's hard for us to say no. But he won't learn anything if you bail him out. All I'm saying is you should think about it. He needs to learn character, not to rely on you for everything. He made a mistake, now it's time for him to figure out how to deal with the consequences."

He shook his head, glanced at her, then sighed. Finally, he stopped, and she puttered to a halt next to him, puffing hard.

"Just like you did with your kids?"

Her brow creased. "What do you mean? I always encourage my children to face the natural consequences of their decisions head on."

"Sure you do," he replied with a huff. "Like the way you gave Sarah and Mick your house at a significant discount. Or the way you handed your business over to Adele, without making her pay a cent for it. You gave her an entire business, an ongoing income she didn't have to earn."

Cindy squared her shoulders. "That's different."

"No, it's not. You love your children, you help them out of jams all the time. I want to do the same for my son. It's no different."

"But it's our money, not just yours," replied Cindy, heat rising up her neck.

"The money you lost when you gave the house and business to your children would've been our money as well if you'd held onto it. But I didn't complain, did I? Because I know how much your children mean to you. Marcus means as much to me."

Cindy sighed. "I know he does, but it isn't the same thing.

Sarah and Mick paid for their house. Adele is working her tail off at the cafe. Besides, the cafe was handed down to me by my parents, so I gave it to Adele. It was an inheritance."

He rubbed both hands over his face. His cheeks were red, his eyes flashed. "It's the same thing, don't try to tell me it's not. I want to help Marcus and Anna buy their first house. Yes, he's made some bad choices, but who hasn't? Certainly, Adele has."

"Let's not go there," snapped Cindy, her head spinning with anger. How dare he bring up Adele's affair. It was something she'd told him in confidence, not for him to use as a weapon against her in an argument.

"Fine, we won't go there. But just so you know — this thing you do, where you act like your children are perfect, and other people's kids are flawed, is irritating at best. I won't put up with you treating Marcus that way. We're married now, so he's your child as well, in a sense. I know he's grown, but he's your family. I treat your children like family, I expect you to do the same for him and Anna."

With a wave of his hand, Athol backed up. "I'm going home. I'll see you there." Head bent forward, shoulders hunched against the afternoon breeze, he marched back down the beach the way they'd come, leaving Cindy behind.

AN HOUR later she was back at the house. Athol was upstairs on the deck outside their bedroom listening to music on his headphones and staring moodily out over the ocean as twilight descended. Cindy pottered around the kitchen, thawing beef for stroganoff and slicing capsicum and onions. She'd give him time to cool off before she broached the subject they'd fought over on the beach.

Already she felt ashamed of what she'd said. She stood by

her words, but they weren't necessary. Marcus was Athol's child, of course he wanted to help him. And as his wife she should stand by his decision. Shouldn't she? She was so confused. After decades of marriage to Andy, a man who rarely included his wife in any of the decisions he made and who kept up a happy facade while plunging her into massive debt, she wasn't sure what was normal and what wasn't. At least Athol had come to her with this, rather than going behind her back to give money away to his son. That was probably what Andy would've done.

The phone in her jeans pocket rang and she tugged it free with a grunt. That took more effort these days, and certainly more than it should. Perhaps she'd already gained weight since the wedding. She'd been happy and she and Athol ate out at restaurants more often than she had when she was single. She'd have to remember to step on the scales the next morning before breakfast. No need to make things worse by doing it so late in the evening when she'd probably scare the life out of herself with the number on the digital screen.

"Hello?" she answered the phone as a question, while holding it against her ear and stirring the sizzling onion in a large, heavy pan.

"Hi Mum, it's Ethan. Are you busy?"

"Hello, sweetheart. Never too busy for you. What's going on?"

He sighed. "You know that Emily and I were supposed to be visiting her second cousins in Tasmania for Christmas?"

She nodded. "Um...yes." The onion was browning too quickly, so she switched off the burner to give Ethan her full attention. She sat at the dining table and leaned on an elbow to stare out over the back garden.

"Well, they've come down with the flu. In the middle of summer. Can you believe it? It snowed there the other day.

Tasmanian weather, huh? Anyway, they caught the flu and both of them are laid up. So, we've had to cancel our flights."

"You're staying in the Cove for Christmas?"

"Yep."

"Well, so are we."

"What?"

She laughed. "We decided yesterday, but I haven't had a chance to call and let you know. Athol and I aren't leaving the country, after all. I'll fill you in on the details when I see you, but let's just say, I'm glad to be staying home, even though I'm disappointed at the same time."

"So, what are we all doing for Christmas Day, then?"

She combed fingers through her hair. It fell into soft waves around her face. "Good question."

* * *

AFTER SHE FINISHED SPEAKING with Ethan, Cindy sat down at the table to write out a shopping list. She wasn't feeling up to shopping alone, but perhaps she could convince Adele to go with her. Now that they were staying home for the holidays, they'd need supplies. Although, how much, and what, depended entirely on what they planned to do. She returned to the kitchen to work on dinner, mulling over the dishes she might serve.

There was no point planning anything until she'd spoken to Sarah. She picked up her phone and dialled Sarah's number. It rang for almost a minute before she finally answered, sleep lacing her voice.

"Hello?"

"You sound tired, love. Everything okay?"

Sarah yawned loudly. "Fine, I fell asleep when I put Leo down for a nap."

"I'm sorry to wake you." Cindy added the sliced beef to the pan and stirred it as it fried.

"No, it's okay. I had to get up and make dinner anyway. How are you feeling, Mum?"

"I'm fine. I wanted to talk to you about Christmas Day."

Sarah yawned again. "Oh?"

"I spoke to Ethan. He and Emily are staying in the Cove now, too. It seems to me we're all going to be in town."

Sarah laughed. "Well, how about that? Here I was thinking you'd all abandoned me, and now everything's changed."

"Is that really what you thought, honey? That I'd abandoned you?"

"I'm only joking, Mum. Although I'm happy you'll see Leo for his first Christmas."

"I am as well. I'll miss seeing Sue and the family but I'm glad I'll be here with you."

"Will you come here, then?" asked Sarah.

"That's what I was calling to talk to you about. Can we do that? Will you cope with us all lobbing in on you at the last minute?"

"It's fine, Mum. I'm looking forward to it."

She hung up with Sarah after talking over the menu and got back to making dinner. Athol appeared at the bottom of the staircase, his face still glum. She hated that they'd fought. Their first argument, and it was over something so important and that'd caused him so much pain. If only she could take back her words, but she didn't know how to without seeming false. He'd know she hadn't changed her mind, he'd see through her attempts.

"I hope you're hungry," she said.

He grunted, searched in one of the cupboards for a mug which he withdrew. Then, went looking for something else.

"Can I help you find something?"

He shook his head. "I feel like a drink, but I don't know if I want coffee or tea."

"How about coffee with eggnog?"

He shrugged. "That sounds nice."

She faced him, a wooden spoon in one hand. "Please forgive me, my love."

He sighed. "For what?"

"For the things I said."

"But you meant them," he retorted. "You haven't changed your mind, have you?"

She inhaled a long breath. "I don't want to talk about it right now. I'd like to have a nice cup of coffee together, then to eat this delicious beef stroganoff I'm preparing. I don't want to fight anymore tonight."

"I guess I can live with that."

She cupped his cheek with one hand. "One thing I've learned after so many years of marriage, arguments can wait until the next day. It doesn't hurt to air them out a bit."

He huffed in a laughing kind of way. "You're right about that. I'm happy to take a break. We can argue more tomorrow." The usual sparkle returned to his eyes. "Let's have some eggnog coffee and forget about it until then."

She switched off the stove top again, filled their coffee cups, and walked hand in hand with Athol outside to the back deck. They sat together in the garden, watching as the sun set beyond the town. Birds twittered and dove around them catching insects for supper. Crickets chirruped and the ocean soothed Cindy's aching heart. Through the open kitchen windows, Christmas music drifted, filling Cindy with a sense of hope. They shouldn't fight over the holidays. If only she could put off the argument forever, but it would come back to them to be dealt with at some point whether she wanted it to or not.

CHAPTER 12

SARAH

*T*he shopping trolley wove back and forth down the aisle of the Foodstore with Sarah clinging onto the handle for dear life. Why she had to find the only trolley with a broken wheel she didn't know. Besides that, there were no others spare. Every person in Emerald Cove seemed to be doing a last-minute holiday shop, and she barely had room to navigate her way down the aisles. With the recalcitrant trolley causing her to narrowly miss people's heels, she bit on the inside of her cheek and grimaced every time it jolted or ran into a shelf. Leo slept soundly against her chest in a sling, his lips slightly parted.

"Sorry!" she called, as the trolley glanced off a woman's hip. The woman glared at her, and Sarah hurried away as fast as she could without mowing anyone else down.

Cheerful Christmas carols boomed through the shop's speaker system, along with the occasional announcement by

Marg in the deli section about a discount on some item or other.

"Don't forget to order your barbecue chooks ahead of time," came Marg's slow drawl through the speakers. "And sliced turkey is fifty percent off for today only."

Sarah pulled the trolley to a halt to stare at the shopping list on her phone. Sweat dripped down her back even with the shop's air conditioning blasting cold air through the store.

Her phone rang, surprising her. It was Adele. She answered with a brusque hello.

"You sound harried," said Adele. "Everything okay?"

"Everything's fine," replied Sarah in a sing-song voice. She sounded so much like her own mother that she clamped her mouth shut in horror. When had that happened? When had she morphed into Mum?

"Wow, that was uncanny," replied Adele.

"What?"

"Nothing, never mind."

Sarah knew exactly what Adele was thinking, although neither of them was willing to admit it. She was living in her mother's house and now she sounded like her. Perhaps the transformation would one day be complete and she'd end up with a blonde bob, working at the Emerald Cafe. She'd *become* Cindy Flannigan. Mick would be so pleased.

"I'm calling to talk to you about Christmas Day."

Sarah resisted the urge to sigh loudly. Everyone had been calling all day long, and every phone call had resulted in the same thing — more people coming to Christmas lunch. She didn't have the heart to tell Mum that Dad and Keisha were coming. Her mother and Dad's girlfriend didn't exactly get along. She didn't know how it would work, with the two of them having to play nice at Christmas time.

"Don't worry, I know you're coming, even though you

didn't call to let me know. I spoke to Mum, and she told me all about it. Ethan and Emily are coming too."

"Oh really?" replied Adele. "That's great. So we'll all be there?"

"Yep. Everyone. Even Dad and Keisha."

"Oh wow. That will be interesting." Adele laughed. "Mum's going to flip."

"Please don't say anything. I don't want to rock the boat. Mum's bringing most of the food."

"You've got to tell her, Sar."

"I know," replied Sarah, still hoping in the pit of her stomach that she didn't have to broach the subject. There were so many people coming to Christmas, perhaps Mum and Keisha didn't have to see each other.

"Anyway, I called to let you know I invited two more people to lunch. I hope that's okay. I made a couple of new friends, and they don't know anyone else in the area. I thought it would be nice to include them in our Christmas celebration. Their names are Samuel and Carlos."

Sarah swallowed hard, blinked twice. "Uh, okay. Thanks for letting me know."

When she hung up the phone, Sarah felt as though she was having a panic attack. Two more people to add to the list. She wasn't even sure how much food she'd need for that many people. In fact, she hadn't sat down to add up the numbers, but it seemed like a lot for one meal. Usually Mum managed all of these types of events. She'd never hosted a big holiday meal before. And she had a newborn, so she was sleep-deprived and seemed utterly incapable of managing a complex thought, let alone mathematical calculations or meal planning.

And of course Adele didn't even consider how her actions might impact on Sarah. She always simply assumed that Sarah would cope with it. Sarah would take care of it. She was the older sister, so she was the responsible one. The one who organised get togethers, prepared the meals, cleaned up afterwards, and generally kept everyone happy. Adele came to family gatherings, sat down with Dad or Ethan, and chatted until her heart was content, while Sarah and Mum rushed around frantically taking care of it all.

It was just how things were. Adele was young. She didn't think much about any of it. Which made sense. Sarah hadn't when she was that age either. Still, it would've been nice for Adele to give her a call and ask first, before she invited two strangers to her Christmas lunch. Normally it wouldn't bother her, but now she wasn't sure she could even manage hosting the immediate family, let alone anyone else. Never mind, there was nothing to be done about it now. She'd simply have to cope. There was no other option.

With a trolley full of groceries, she navigated her way to the checkout. The broken wheel sent the trolley in the wrong direction, and she had to use every ounce of strength in her still-recovering abdomen to try to keep it on course. With Leo strapped to her chest, it was all she could do to steer, since her arms had to reach around the baby to clutch onto the trolley handle. She shoved the trolley forward, careful not to bump the sleeping baby.

One by one, she hurried each item out of the trolley onto the conveyor belt. The girl behind the register waited, with sleepy eyes glancing at the watch on her wrist every few seconds and acting as though she was about to sigh. Sarah shot her a tortured smile. She'd never realised before how difficult shopping could be with a baby in a sling and every single part of her body pushed to the point of exhaustion. All she wanted to do was lie down in bed, turn the air conditioner on full blast, pull up the covers, and sleep for days. And it didn't help that Mick was working on a large renovation outside of town that had him out until all hours of the night, seven days a week. The client wanted the project finished by Christmas. Mick and his team were doing everything they could to make that happen. But that meant Sarah was on her own with Leo most of the time. She needed Mick now more than ever, and even though he was making the money that kept their little family afloat, it still felt unfair to her at times.

Tears pricked her eyes, and she fought them back, swallowing them down with a sob. She wouldn't cry in public. The last thing she needed now was to humiliate herself in front of a bunch of tourists and a teenaged girl with blue fingernail polish and bleached blonde hair who was counting down the minutes until her shift ended.

Just then, Leo squawked. Sarah's entire body tensed. No, he couldn't wake up now. Not yet. She was so close to getting the groceries onto the conveyor belt. Halfway there. If he could simply stay asleep for a few more minutes, she'd be out of there and could feed him in the car.

She bounced in place, shushing quietly while she continued reaching into the trolley. But Leo was having none of it. He squalled and squirmed, his cries soon reaching an ear-splitting crescendo. Sarah grimaced, biting down on her lower lip, and begged him silently to wait. She couldn't bear the thought of abandoning her shopping trolley full of things they'd need for Christmas. Then she'd have to come back tomorrow and start all over again. But tomorrow was Christmas Eve and she'd planned on cooking and cleaning. There was no way she could get everything done if she left now.

The girl with bleached hair stared at her, eyes vacant. Sarah shrugged. "I guess I'm gonna have to go. Sorry." She pulled her purse and Leo's nappy bag out of the trolley and slung one over each shoulder.

"I'll put these through for you," the girl replied. "Don't worry about it."

Sarah gaped. It wasn't what she'd expected to hear from the bored looking teenager.

The girl picked at a fingernail, flicking blue paint onto the floor. "Happens all the time," she mumbled. "Don't worry about it."

Sarah offered a wobbly smile. "Okay, thanks. That helps me a lot. I'll be right back."

She rushed to the front of the shop where they'd installed a small but clean parents' room and pushed the door open. Once inside, she slumped into a feeding chair, tugged Leo free, and fed him. His screams stopped almost immediately, with only a whimper every few moments. Tears spilled from Sarah's eyes onto her cheeks as she watched him. Tension formed knots in her shoulders and a rock in her gut.

It was all too hard. She couldn't do it. She reached for her mobile phone in her purse and leaned her head back on the chair.

"Mum?"

"Hi, honey, what's going on?"

"I can't do it," she sobbed.

Cindy's voice rose with alarm. "What's wrong, Sarah? Tell me…has something happened?"

"No, nothing's happened. Everyone's fine. I mean, no one's hurt or anything like that. But I'm a mess. I can't do it all. I thought I could — they sell us that lie, you know?"

"What lie, honey?" asked Mum, her tone soft and comforting as the panic faded from her voice.

"That we can have it all. Do it all. We can't. It's too much."

Mum laughed. "Oh, that lie. Yep. You can't have it all, not at the same time anyway. You can have different things at different times, but you can't have everything at once. That's now how life works, I'm afraid."

Sarah groaned, as tears wet her cheeks. "Why didn't anyone tell me that?"

"Oh, honey, I guess I thought you witnessed it firsthand in me. I've never been able to juggle all the moving parts very well. I did the best I could, but I always let someone down — either the cafe, your father, you kids or myself. There's a cost to everything."

Leo had settled and was feeding happily now. Sarah stroked his head. His beautiful eyes were shut, his cheeks working furiously. He was so perfect. But how could something so perfect make so much noise? She giggled in the midst of her tears. Great, now she was losing her mind. Laughing and crying at the same time. Stressed, anxious, lonely, and yet perfectly happy and content. What was wrong with her?

"I think I'm falling apart, Mum," she said. "I was grocery shopping, and Leo wouldn't stop crying. I had to leave the groceries at the register and sprint to the parents' room. And I don't know how I'll manage Christmas lunch with everything that's going on."

Mum sighed. "Oh, honey, I didn't realise you were struggling so hard. You show the rest of us such a brave face. But it's okay to be vulnerable every now and then, you know."

Sarah sighed, wiping her tears with the back of her hand. "I know, Mum. I want to be strong, really, I do. But I don't think I can be right now. I'm so tired."

"Of course you are, love. Forget about Christmas lunch, we'll have it at my place. You come along with your beautiful family and don't worry about a thing. The rest of us will take care of it all."

Tears squeezed once again from Sarah's eyes as relief washed over her. "Thanks, Mum. That takes such a load off my mind. I'm sorry — I know that puts pressure on you."

"I can handle it, honey. Besides, I have Athol and Adele to help me out."

Sarah sniffled, then searched in Leo's nappy bag for a tissue. She couldn't find one, but there was a packet of wet wipes. She pulled one free and blew her nose into it. It was cold against her skin. She pulled another one out and wiped her hot face with it, blotting her tears gently.

"Thanks again, Mum. I'll do Christmas Eve dinner, since I'm only planning a barbecue. That should be easy enough. Although if Mick's schedule doesn't change I may order take-away instead. And I've got some groceries I can drop by your place on my way home if you need them for Christmas lunch."

"That would be wonderful, thanks, sweetie."

"Oh," continued Sarah, "by the way, I forgot to mention one thing."

"What's that?" asked Mum, her usual sing-song tone returning and making Sarah smile.

"Dad and Keisha are coming to Christmas lunch."

CHAPTER 13

24TH DECEMBER

ADELE

*T*he shopping centre was chaotic and loud. Christmas music crooned from speakers across the wide ceiling. Archways were festooned with wreaths and garlands. Adele scrambled up an escalator, her purse swinging over one shoulder. Puffing slightly, she surveyed the row of shops on the next level. Where should she go first?

She hadn't bought gifts for anyone yet and stress gnawed at her gut. She had to find something special for every important person in her life in one afternoon. Was that even possible?

And what about the staff? Was she expected to buy them gifts? She still wasn't sure how all that worked. With everything going on in her life lately, gift buying had completely slipped her mind. Running the cafe took up most of her waking hours. She never realised how much work it would be to manage the place and was amazed at how well her mother had done it for so many years. She must've been exhausted much of the time, and yet she'd been such a wonderful mother to Adele, Sarah and Ethan. She wondered whether it was simply youthful ignorance overlooking the stress her mother lived under, or if Mum had simply hidden it really well.

She wandered into *The Body Shop* and perused the shelves. Perhaps she could get something decadent for Sarah. Although she had no idea if her sister enjoyed the occasional bath bomb or face mask. She wasn't really the type, in Adele's experience. But motherhood might've changed that. Still, a bath bomb wasn't a personal gift. And the sisterly bond they shared was an important one. She should buy something that reflected that. Although, what kind of gift could express how much she appreciated and loved her sister? Perhaps it was asking too much of a gift to do something like that.

A strand of blonde hair fell into her eyes as she studied a shampoo shaped like a bar of soap, but with glitter. She put down the shampoo, shook her head, and marched out of the shop. It was too much, completely overwhelming. She wasn't someone who liked to shop, especially under a time crunch. She hesitated, threw her arms in the air, and spun on her heel to go back to the shop.

By the time she'd bought Sarah a bar of glitter shampoo and Mum a neon pink bath bomb, she was ready for a cup of coffee and something very sweet to eat. Her energy levels had taken a dive as she'd been on her feet all morning at the café, and she needed a pick up.

With the small paper bag swinging from one hand, reminding her just how much shopping she had yet to do, she hurried along the wide but very crowded aisle to her favourite coffee place, dodging pedestrians as she went. She didn't see the man in her path until she'd run directly into his strong, hard back. She grunted and grabbed for her nose. It stung where it'd impacted his shoulder blade. With a frown she stepped back, wondering why he'd stopped directly in the middle of the thoroughfare. He turned to face her, and she gasped, still clutching her nose.

"Carlos?"

"Are you okay?" he asked, reaching out to her.

He guided her free of the crowd to a small bench seat against a glass railing. She sat as she massaged her nose. It didn't seem to be injured, although it still smarted a little.

"What were you doing stopping like that?" she asked, in irritation.

He shrugged. "Trying to figure out where I'm going. I don't know what to get Tito for Christmas."

"I bet he'd love a nice jacket, or a pair of gum boots for fishing. Oh, or a wide-brimmed hat." Why was it so easy for her to come up with ideas for a man she barely knew, but when considering her own family her mind was completely blank?

He smiled as he lowered himself to the seat beside her. "Those are great ideas. Are you sure you're okay? I'm sorry I was in the way."

"I'm sorry I ran into you. And yes, I'm fine. Thanks. You?"

He nodded. "Perfectly fine. And now I have ideas for what to get Tito. So, thank you."

She sighed. "I know how it feels. I'm at a complete loss for what to buy my family. My sister, Sarah, and I are close. So you'd think I'd have some idea of what she might like. I can't get her something she needs, or anything for the baby — that's what everyone else will be doing. I want to get her a gift she'll appreciate, that's just for her." She shook her head. "But I'm coming up empty. All I got so far is this?"

She dug the bar of shampoo out of the bag and held it up. It looked even more pitiful on its own now she was away from the shop and the other matching products.

His brow furrowed. "What is that? Is it soap?"

She groaned. "No, it's shampoo. See, it's a terrible gift. She won't even know what it is. Plus, it's tiny. I need to get her something else."

"Isn't she a new mum? You mentioned that she's feeling overwhelmed, when you called to tell us the new location for Christmas lunch."

"She is — apparently she's not getting much sleep. I think I'm going to offer to spend the night there tonight, so maybe she can sleep in tomorrow while I get up with the baby."

"That's a great idea for a gift," replied Carlos. "That and a massage."

Adele's eyes widened. "A massage. Yes, she'd love that. I know she used to get them when she lived in Sydney, but I don't think she's had one in ages."

"Plus, it won't give her blue hair," added Carlos. "Come on, if we shop together maybe we'll get it finished sooner."

"I was about to have a coffee, to steel myself for the rest of the afternoon," said Adele.

"Perfect, I could use a coffee too," replied Carlos, his eyes sparkling.

Adele walked beside him to the cafe, a smile tugging at her lips. She was glad she'd dressed up a little more than she had done lately, before heading out to the shops. She'd felt more energised than usual, had curled her hair and donned a navy, strapless dress with neutral flats. Usually she didn't have the energy, especially after a long day working at the cafe. But the past few days she'd begun to feel a spark of life return. As though she was finally emerging from the post-breakup slump.

She could tell by the way he looked at her that Carlos

liked the dress. And now she wouldn't have to sit at the cafe alone. She'd been thinking about him all day, wondering what he was doing and if she'd get a chance to see him before Christmas. And here he was. It couldn't be a coincidence, the way she kept running into him. It must be fate. There was no other logical explanation.

* * *

TWO HOURS LATER, Adele and Carlos had completed their Christmas shopping. Adele had a lot more people to buy for, with her large family, her staff, and her friends in the Cove. So, Carlos made suggestions and held bags, while she scurried here and there, hoping her credit card wouldn't max out before she was done.

"I really don't think I can buy anything else," she said, with a sigh. "I'm fairly sure my credit card is close to the limit, and I probably need fuel on the way home."

Carlos reached for the bag of items she'd purchased in one of the many decor shops that were dotted throughout the shopping centre. "I don't know how you'll keep track of everything. My head is spinning with all of the names and gifts."

She laughed. "I'll figure it out. Thank you so much for your help."

"It's not over yet. I'll carry some of your bags to the car. Otherwise, I'm afraid I'll hear about a woman being swallowed by her shopping bags on the news later tonight."

Adele couldn't help smiling all the way to the car. The more she got to know Carlos, the more he made her laugh. He'd seemed so shy and reserved the first time they'd met. Now, he was laughing, talking, cracking jokes, and opening up to her in a way that was completely endearing.

As he pushed the last bag of shopping into the boot of her hatchback, he sighed. "So, I guess that's it."

"Yep. Thanks again." She didn't want him to leave. But she couldn't think of anything else to say to get him to stay. They'd talked for two straight hours, as they scoured the shops for just the right gifts to purchase. About politics, philosophy, her career and where it was and wasn't going, and his career and how far he still had to go before becoming a psychologist.

She'd had so much fun getting to know him. And now she had to go home alone to her flat and wrap the gifts before rushing to Sarah's for Christmas Eve dinner with family.

"I suppose I'll see you tomorrow then," he said.

She nodded. "I'm looking forward to it." She shut the boot of the car and opened the driver's side door. There was something going on between them. Something she couldn't ignore. But there was also the issue of her affair, a relationship that had only recently ended.

"I'd like to call you sometime, if that's okay." He pushed his hands into the pockets of his shorts.

"That'd be nice. I'd like that too."

He grinned. "Great. I really like you, Adele. I think we should get to know each other better."

She swallowed. He deserved to know the truth. To know what she'd done, what she was in the process of ending. "There's something I should tell you."

He arched an eyebrow. "Oh?"

"It's about my last relationship."

"You're not married or anything, are you?"

She laughed awkwardly. "No, not me. But he was."

"Wow. I wasn't expecting that.'

"I should never have been involved with him. We worked together and I fell for him so fast. I was young, right out of school, and he was older and married. He seemed like the perfect guy. We were both pilots, we had so much in common. Then, when I was already head over heels, I found out he was married." She explained the situation to Carlos. The relationship they'd shared, the lies he'd told. And how she'd moved back to the Cove to get away from him and start afresh. To put the pieces of her life back together.

He leaned against her car, his arms crossed over his chest and listened, nodding every now and then but otherwise staying quiet. His eyes were soft, full of compassion. She didn't see any judgement, although the nerves in her stomach tumbled over each other as she searched his expression for it. She couldn't stand it if he hated or judged her for what she'd done. She judged herself harshly enough for it, but if he did — she wasn't sure she could take seeing disgust or shock in his eyes without crying.

"So, it's over between us. I've left him behind. He was calling but I've blocked his number. Mum kept telling me I should do it, but I've had this strange connection to him that I haven't been able to shake. I didn't want to cut him out of my life completely, couldn't bring myself to do it. But it's done. I won't talk to him again." She chewed nervously on a fingernail. "Say something, please."

"I'm sorry you went through all of that. I think you're really strong to be able to walk away, move away in fact, and start your life over again. That's a big deal." His brown eyes fixed on hers. They were deep, soft, and she wanted to sink into their depths.

"Thank you," she whispered. "You don't think I'm horrible?"

He shook his head. "No, of course not. You fell in love, what's so horrible about that?"

"But he was married."

"You didn't know that."

"No…not at first."

"And now you're moving on."

She smiled. "I am. And I'm glad to be back in the Cove, if I'm honest. I wanted so much to get away and stand on my own two feet that I didn't much think about everything I'd be giving up when I left. But now I'm back, I'm loving being around my family and having the cafe. Plus, I can surf or swim in the ocean anytime I like. I don't have to worry about saltwater crocodiles or deadly jellyfish. It's great."

Carlos stepped closer to her and reached for her hand. He held it in his, stroking the back of it with his thumb in a circular motion. "I'm glad you came back to the Cove as well."

She bit down on her lower lip as happiness surged through her body, pushing away the unshed tears that'd sat at the back of her throat while she spoke.

"It's all going to be okay," he said. "You're strong, and you have a good heart. So, I know that it will work out, in the end."

His arms enveloped her in a hug and she leaned into him. The strength of his embrace, the warmth of his body, it soothed her to her core. She believed his words. It would be okay. She'd get through this; she'd already taken the steps to do it. And she was rebuilding the life for herself that she wanted. A stray tear wound its way down her cheek, and she brushed it away with her sleeve.

"Is that your clinical opinion?" she asked.

They laughed together, the sound drowning out the small voice deep down inside that told her there was something wrong with her and replacing it with a voice of hope.

* * *

ADELE'S THOUGHTS wandered as she rode the elevator up to the top floor of her apartment complex. The feel of Carlos's arms around her still lingered and she smiled as she recalled the way he'd comforted her. She recalled when she first saw him helping the elderly lady with her shopping trolly. She'd thought about how she never met men like him. But now she'd met him and he was everything she'd dreamed he might be. Kind, thoughtful, strong and yet gentle. He cared about her, what she was going through, wanted to know what she thought about everything. They hadn't run out of things to talk about, and the conversation was easy.

As she walked through the front door into her unit, arms laden with shopping bags, her phone rang. She set the bags on the floor, kicked the front door shut and pulled the phone from her purse. She didn't recognise the number, it was a Darwin area code. What if it was Antoine? She'd blocked his number, but perhaps he was trying again from another number.

With a flash of anger, she answered. "Hello?"

"Is this Adele Flannigan?" The voice was unfamiliar, tinged by a soft accent.

Her anger dissipated. "Yes, this is Adele."

"Adele, my name is Lee Chin from Hong Kong Airways. I hoped you might have a minute to speak with me."

Adele slapped a hand to her forehead. She'd forgotten all about the invitation to interview with the Hong Kong airline. With so much going on in her life, the hectic schedule of the cafe, and the tumult of her family life, she hadn't given it another thought since Becky told her about the letter.

"Yes, of course."

"We have openings for several pilots, since our airline is expanding. I was given your name as a recommendation. If you're interested, I'd like to set up a time to sit down and chat about the openings."

She inhaled a quick breath. "I appreciate you calling me, but I have to decline. I've moved to Emerald Cove, and I'm

not looking for a position as a pilot at this time. But I'll definitely let you know if that changes."

As she hung up the phone, nerves twisted in the pit of her
gut. Was she really ready to give up the career she'd worked
so hard to build? Her recent conversation with Antoine had
rattled her. She felt sick to her stomach at the thought of
returning to Darwin any time soon.

For now, at least, she needed a break from her past. There
was nothing to stop her returning to work as a pilot in the
future. But it wasn't something she wanted to do now. That
resolved, she undressed, stepped into the shower and turned
on the tap, letting the cool water wash away the sweat, stress
and fatigue of the day.

CHAPTER 14

CARLOS

*T*ito's house sparkled and blinked in the dim light with brightly coloured twinkle lights. Carlos wondered where Tito had gotten them from and why he hadn't waited for Carlos to help him hang them. It would be just like Tito to climb a ladder to hang the lights and take a fall because he wasn't being careful. Carlos shook his head as he rode his bicycle up to the front of Tito's house and pulled it to a stop.

The sun hadn't set yet, but a few clouds hugged the horizon making twilight earlier than usual. Carlos climbed off his bike and pushed it up the curb. Sweat soaked his back under his backpack. He'd packed a casserole dish filled with empanadas plus a small wrapped gift of cigars he'd bought for Tito. Yaya had made his grandfather quit smoking decades ago, but every now and then he hid a good cigar in his pocket and sneaked outside to smoke it. Carlos knew his little secret and this year he'd bought him the best cigars he could afford so they could smoke in the courtyard together after dinner. Or maybe they'd stroll down to the beach and walk on the sand under the moonlight, since the weather was so fine.

Crickets chirruped, and in a stand of gums at the end of the street a kookaburra laughed. It set off a chorus of calls that echoed loud through the neighbourhood. Carlos leaned his bike against the garage wall, then skipped up the front steps and opened the door. Tito never locked the door. It was a habit he'd had for as long as Carlos could remember. Whenever he asked him about it, Tito only scoffed at the idea of locking up.

"Australia is the safest place in the world. Who would need to lock their door here?" he'd say with a wave of his hand.

No one loved his adopted country more than Tito. He and his family had fled to Australia with a drug cartel chasing them. The head of the cartel put a bounty on Tito's head when he'd refused to work for him. Tito had also angered the cartel when he'd run for local political office, with a campaign slogan promising to make changes for a better community by cleaning up the drug trade. The drug cartel came after him before he had the chance to be elected and they'd run as far as they could without falling off the planet, as Tito always said. He laughed when he said it, but Carlos knew how much pain his grandfather felt over leaving behind his country, extended family and friends to start again in a strange and distant land, where he didn't know the language.

Carlos had heard the stories time and time again over the years. It was a life he'd never known, but one his grandparents couldn't forget. They wouldn't let him forget where he'd come from either, even if he'd never lived there. And now that it was only him and Tito left, his grandfather made sure to remind him of his heritage whenever he had the chance.

"Hello! Tito," he called as he stepped into the house.

The scent of cinnamon and nutmeg filled his nostrils, and he noted a lit candle on the coffee table. It smelled like Christmas and added to the cheer in the house, along with Tito's decorations and the blinking of the lights outside through the window. The air-conditioning cooled him immediately and he breathed in a sigh of relief. He wasn't running the air at his own flat since it cost too much and he still hadn't landed a job yet. Although, he had some prospects at a few places around town. He figured he should have managed to secure some kind of employment before he headed back to university in February. If he didn't, he might have to ask Tito to help him pay the rent before then.

"Is that you, Carlos?" called back Tito from the kitchen. "Come in here. I tried making Christmas cider, but I'm not sure I got it right."

Carlos found Tito standing over the stove top stirring something in a large pot. The scent of cinnamon was even stronger in the kitchen than it had been in the living room.

"Wow, that smells delicious," said Carlos.

Tito held out a small plastic cup with a handle. "Here, have a taste and tell me what you think. I'm trying to embrace the whole Christmas spirit thing. And since it's our first Christmas without your grandmother, I figured we should put in a little effort to make it special."

Carlos sipped the cider and smiled. "Perfect. Now it needs rum."

Tito grinned, held up a bottle of dark rum and set it back on the bench by the stove. "Way ahead of you, my boy."

Tito poured each of them a mug of cider spiked with rum, and then checked on the pot of ajiaco bubbling on top of the stove. He took a sip of cider, stirred the soup, then turned it off.

"Let's sit outside for a few minutes before we eat. The weather is finally cooling off."

Outside, the humidity enveloped them the moment they stepped onto the porch. They sat side-by-side in two folding chairs and looked out across the courtyard to a vine-covered trellis that was hung with sweet-scented white flowers and had overrun one side of the yard. Long shadows crawled across the cracked and faded tiles where weeds had found their place and lifted the edges of the tiles.

Carlos sipped his drink in silence and slapped at a mosquito that buzzed by his ear.

"I want us to take a moment to be thankful," said Tito.

Carlos glanced at him, gave a brief nod. "Of course."

"We have lost so much, sometimes it's hard to remember what we still have. I know it is for me. But we have each other."

"Very true. We have each other," echoed Carlos. "And I'm grateful for you, Tito."

"If I didn't have you, I'd be sitting here on my own. And that's no way to live."

Carlos agreed. He couldn't imagine spending Christmas on his own, but without Tito that was exactly where he'd be. Although Adele had invited them to spend the day with her family tomorrow, that was a nicety that wouldn't always be offered. Most years, Christmas involved family and no one else. It was something he'd fretted over as a child — everyone else he knew spent the holidays with cousins, aunts, uncles, parents, grandparents. They'd return to the neighbourhood the next day with tales of trips to the beach, fishing for bream, waterskiing behind a speed boat, barbecues and water balloon fights. While he'd spent the day sitting with Tito and

Yaya alone in their house, eating until he thought the button on his pants would burst. After the meal they'd listen to Colombian music while they reminisced about the old days back in Colombia until Yaya made him dance with her. He'd dance until he could barely stand, then he'd make an excuse to escape to his bedroom, and when he peeked through the bedroom door he'd glimpse Tito and Yaya dancing slow, cheek-to-cheek, whispering to each other and laughing.

Now, he didn't want anything more than to spend the day with Tito. He wished Yaya was still with them, but there was nothing that could be done about it. What was in the past, was gone forever. That was what Tito always said after they'd spent the day chewing over all the things they'd left behind when they ran for their lives in the middle of the night. We can't look back. We must move forward.

"That's what I want to talk to you about," continued Tito, pulling Carlos out of his reminiscence.

"Okay."

"I won't be around forever, you know."

"I know that," replied Carlos, scratching his head. "But you're here now."

"Yes, I am. But I don't want you to be alone for the rest of your life when I'm gone."

"We've talked about this before, Tito." Carlos resisted the urge to roll his eyes. Here it comes — the when are you going to get married and settle down conversation.

"We've talked about it, I know. But have you listened to me? You're so focused on your career, you seem to think of nothing else. You study, you work, you take care of me, but where is the life, the fun? You're a young man, you should be enjoying yourself, meeting other young people, spending time out and about. You should be dating beautiful young women instead of doing my gardening."

Carlos rubbed a hand over his face. "*Someone* has to do your gardening."

"True, but perhaps we can live with a few weeds. I want you to be happy."

"I am happy," protested Carlos. And even if he wasn't, what could be done about it? No one can force happiness.

"No, you're not happy. You're existing. There's a difference."

"Is there?" he sighed. "I'm sorry, Tito. I'm doing the best I can."

"I know you are, mijo. I only want you to think about more."

"Well, I went on a date. Does that count?"

"A date? When, with who?"

Carlos grinned. "With Adele."

"When was this date, and why didn't I know anything about it?" Tito leaned forward in his chair, his bushy eyebrows drawn together like an arrowhead.

"Yesterday. I didn't tell you about it because it wasn't planned. We ran into each other and spent the afternoon together. I asked if I could call her, and she said yes."

Tito's full lips pulled into a broad smile. "That is good news. You had a nice time, no?"

"It was great. We really connected. She's a lot of fun."

"And beautiful," agreed Tito.

Carlos's cheeks warmed. "Yes, and beautiful. Of course."

"I like her. I'm glad we'll see her tomorrow. Good for you, mijo."

"Thanks Tito."

"So, you'll think about what I said?"

Carlos shook his head in exasperation. "I'll think about it. Don't worry about me. I'm going to be fine, Tito."

"But I do worry. Loneliness is no way for a young man to live."

"You'll be around for a long time yet, Tito." Carlos swallowed a mouthful of cider.

"No one knows how long they have on this earth." Tito tutted, his tongue clicking softly.

"True."

"Life is short, you should grab it with both hands and find whatever joy you can while it lasts." Tito's voice faded to a whisper and the intensity in his gaze brought a lump to Carlo's throat. He knew what Tito meant — his grandfather had everything in Colombia: a lovely home, a beautiful family, good friends, a life full of joy. And all that had ended in a single night when they'd left it all behind. Then he'd lost his daughter too young, and his wife to cancer years later. He knew all about the fragility of life and the fleeting nature of happiness.

Carlos knew what it was he wanted from life. The one thing he'd never had — a complete family. He longed to find a woman he could love, who would love him in return, and to build a life together. He wanted desperately to have a home packed to the rafters with children, love, and happiness. It was the dream of his heart that he rarely ever thought about or allowed to rise to the surface of his consciousness. Instead, he'd focused all his attention on getting through each day, on doing the best that he could in his chosen career, and to being an attentive grandson. But now there was Adele, and the hope of his longing stirred deep in his gut. She was the kind of woman he could imagine building a life with. He only hoped she felt the same way.

CHAPTER 15

CINDY

he music was turned up too high. Cindy could barely hear herself think. She wiped a stray strand of hair from her eyes and smeared flour across her cheek. It wafted down to the bench top and made her sneeze. She covered the sneeze with her arm, turning away from the bench, then studied the slab of dough with dismay. She'd sneezed close to the bread dough. She was making a twisted fruit bread for Christmas breakfast and now she should probably toss the entire thing out.

With a sigh, she wiped her cheek again and, wide-eyed in horror at herself, shuffled from the kitchen to sneeze in the living room. Anxiety twisted in her gut. There was far too much to do in too short a time. Why had she offered to host Christmas at the last moment? She'd been unwell and, even though she felt much better now, she shouldn't have taken on so much. But Sarah needed her, and whenever her children were sinking, she was the first to dive in to rescue them from turgid waters, no matter if it cost her.

"What was I thinking?" she asked Athol, who stood poised over the mantle on a ladder, a wreath in his hands and a nail between his lips.

He set down the wreath and climbed from the ladder to fetch a hammer from the coffee table. "You'll have to be more specific, I'm afraid my love."

She pressed her hands to her hips. "We weren't even supposed to be in town for the holidays, so I hadn't prepared. Now, I've got to get everything ready at the last moment. The house is a disaster, the food isn't cooked, and I just sneezed on the twisted fruit loaf." She wanted to cry, her throat ached, and her head felt a little dizzy from the new medication she was taking.

Athol walked to her and took her in his arms. She pressed against his chest, as his arms enveloped her with warmth. "Never mind all that. The kids are coming to see us. Not a clean house. And whatever we serve will be fine. Don't get worked up — we know what matters and so does the family."

She relaxed in his arms. He was right. For so many years she'd striven for the perfect Christmas decorations and meals. Her imperfect marriage had caused her so much sorrow, she'd tried to hide her shame under a layer of perfection. But now she knew those things didn't matter, since she had Athol and her children, even little Leo this year. And that was what mattered. She shouldn't let anything interrupt her peace and the joy of the holiday season.

With a smile, she pulled away from Athol to look into his deep brown eyes. "When did you get so wise?"

"It comes with the grey hair," he replied, tugging at his locks.

She laughed. "Mine's not so grey yet, so maybe it'll come to me as well."

"I don't know. You don't wear glasses either, and I think they're part of the equation." He peered at her over the top of his spectacles. "You may have to settle for mediocre wisdom since you're still too young and beautiful for real wisdom."

She slapped playfully at his arm. "Oh, stop it. You do go on."

"Now don't keep interrupting me, wife. I'm under strict orders to get these decorations hung, and if you continue to distract me like this, I might have to carry you up those stairs."

"Carry me?" She laughed.

He grinned. "Well, follow you at a march, at the very least. I could probably drag you in a pinch."

She feigned outrage. "Athol Miller, are you calling me fat?"

"Never, my dear. I'd better get up this ladder before I find myself in real trouble." He winked and climbed the ladder.

Joy bubbled inside as she watched her husband hanging the wreath and humming along to the Christmas tunes playing on the sound system. The friendship and love she shared with Athol were things she'd never truly had with Andy. She and Andy had a lot of fun together, and he'd been charming and charismatic in a way that made her heart race. But at the same time, she'd never known when he was being truthful, what he was hiding, or who he might be with when she couldn't reach him on the phone at night. It'd left her with a pit in her stomach and a chest full of anxiety for many of the years they'd been together, something she was grateful to have left behind.

She hurried back to the kitchen, a smile still tickling her lips, and got to work on a new batch of bread. There was a spring in her step, and she wasn't worried about getting it all done on time. They'd head over to Sarah's for Christmas Eve dinner soon, so she'd get as much done before then as she could manage. But she wouldn't let it make her anxious again. Athol was right — what really mattered was that the family would be together. They might be lacking space in the new house, and the food might not be up to her usual standard. But they'd be together and that would make the holiday special. Nothing could ruin her holiday spirit now.

There was a loud knock at the front door, but she barely heard it above the music. Athol would get it. It was probably the neighbours wanting them to turn down the music. And she would, if only she knew where the remote was hidden. Where had Athol left it? She scanned the kitchen and then wandered into the living room, a frown creasing her brow. Where could it be?

There it was. On the bookshelf next to the row of mysteries. Why had he left it there of all places?

She shook her head and reached for it, then turned down the music. There were voices at the front door. Athol was talking to someone and had let them into the house. Her eyes narrowed. Who would be visiting on Christmas Eve?

Athol stepped into the living room, his cheeks a suspicious shade of red. "Look who it is, my love."

Andy and Keisha followed him into the room. Andy marched over and wrapped her in a tight hug. He kissed her cheek, then laughed.

"You're a little tense there, Cindy. Everything okay?"

Keisha stood beside Athol, surveying the room down the bridge of her nose. She sniffed. "What is that smell?"

"Hello, Andy, hi, Keisha. I'm making bread. What are the two of you doing here?"

"That's a fine welcome," replied Andy with a laugh, as he threw himself into an armchair. "We wanted to celebrate with our friends on this wonderful evening."

"But aren't we all going to Sarah and Mick's?" Athol shifted uncomfortably from foot to foot. His lips formed a thin straight line as though he were holding in something he didn't wish to say, but that was determined to burst from his mouth.

No doubt the thoughts in his head went something along the lines of *get out of this house you cheating scumbag*, but he was too polite to say it out loud. Still, she could dream. The thought brought a smile to her lips.

"We're fumigating," replied Keisha in response, as she lowered herself tentatively onto the couch.

"Oh," replied Cindy, still not understanding. "Fleas?"

"Ugh, no," said Keisha. "Termites."

"Yep, got termites at the house, I'm afraid," added Andy. "They say we can't stay there tonight. Might not be able to go back for a few days, actually. So, we decided to drop by and see our good friends, Cindy and Athol. What better place for us to stay, than with family."

Cindy's heart dropped into her gut. Did he say stay? Surely, he didn't mean it. She glanced at Athol and noted the red tone of his face. His gaze met hers as reality dawned.

Andy and Keisha intended to live in their home for the next few days. Which meant they'd be staying for Christmas. Cindy's stomach twisted into a knot. Suddenly the room felt very small. She wandered into the kitchen and claimed a chair, resting her chin on one fist.

"Stay?" she whispered to herself.

Before long, Andy and Keisha followed her. Keisha eyed the bread dough, her nose wrinkling. Andy grinned dumbly and sat beside Cindy, linking his hands behind his head to lean back in the chair.

"Now this is the life, Christmas with friends in the best place on earth," he said.

"I'll have to talk to Athol," she began.

Andy waved a hand. "Athol won't mind. The two of you will barely even notice we're here."

It was going be a long Christmas.

* * *

PANS of warm bread sat cooling on the bench top. Cindy mixed the last of the cucumber slices into the fresh salad, then covered the bowl with a beeswax lid and set it aside. She sprinkled parmesan cheese on top of the trays of lasagna. The lasagna was cold, had spent the night in the fridge, but she could heat it up at Sarah's. She'd always found that day-old lasagna was infinitely more delicious than freshly cooked. Finally, she covered the rice salad and warm potato salad with beeswax lids and called for Athol to help carry everything to the car.

She and Athol walked to the garage, carrying the prepared food with them. In the living room, Andy and Keisha sat side by side in armchairs. Keisha's eyes were shut, her feet resting on the raised footstool. Andy flicked through a magazine.

"You got any of that eggnog lying around?" he asked Cindy as she marched past.

She inhaled a quick breath. "Yes, I do. Would you like a glass?"

"That'd be great, love," he replied with a grin.

Her nostrils flared but she reminded herself that they were guests. She wasn't married to him any longer, yet somehow he still managed to grate on her nerves even more than he had when they were. It was infuriating the way he and his girlfriend had lobbed in on them on Christmas Eve, without so much as a phone call to ask permission. And ever since they arrived, the two of them had expected Cindy to wait on them hand and foot, as though she was their servant.

Andy had been vague in his estimation of how long the fumigation might take, and Cindy knew him well enough to know she couldn't really trust any timeframe he gave her. He hadn't expressed remorse over setting up the fumigation of his home over the holidays. But she wasn't at all surprised, it was just like him to be so disorganised and thoughtless. He hadn't considered the fact that she was experiencing a health crisis, or at the very least a health situation. Had he asked her about how she was feeling? Of course not. He expected her to wait on him, like she always had, and to smile about it, no matter whether her head spun or her back ached. The worst of it was that Athol had barely spoken a word to her since they'd arrived. She had the distinct feeling her husband wasn't happy with the situation or with her. She wished he'd speak up and do something about it.

Never mind, it wouldn't last. All she had to do was get through this evening and tomorrow, and she'd be free. Surely, they wouldn't expect to stay longer than that.

She poured a glass of eggnog for both Andy and Keisha, then hurried to make up the guest room and dress for dinner. By the time she got back downstairs, she found everyone standing by the front door waiting on her, ready to leave.

"We'll miss the drinks if we don't hurry," said Keisha, glancing at her watch with a sigh.

Cindy bit back a retort and resorted to her sing-song voice. "Let's get going then, shall we?"

"I hope you're bringing a bottle of the Scotch I love," said Andy to Athol, as they headed out the front door.

"I wasn't going to," replied Athol, reaching into his pocket for his keys.

"We could share a glass together," added Andy, hesitating on the threshold. "I've missed the stuff. Truth be told, Keisha doesn't like me drinking it. Says it's bad for my waistline, but then it's Christmas, after all. And if you can't indulge a little bit at the holidays, when can you?"

The sun hung over the horizon. The heat of the outdoors had already caused a trickle of sweat at the top of Cindy's back that wound its way down her spine beneath her cotton, floral dress. She tapped a toe on the ground in her nude pumps. "I suppose it wouldn't hurt."

Athol shot her a look of irritation. "I suppose not."

He didn't want to do it, that much was clear. Athol was usually so patient and easy going. But he was obviously irritated with the situation. And she couldn't blame him. She'd done everything she could to get ready on time, but their new houseguests had claimed so much of her attention she'd been thrown off course in her tightly planned schedule. And she hadn't given herself time to think about the fact that Andy and Keisha planned to stay with her and Athol. Their first Christmas as a married couple and this was their reward. Would she ever escape her ex-husband?

Athol returned into the house, no doubt on the search for a bottle of whiskey. Cindy wasn't sure they had one, since it wasn't something Athol drank often. Now that she thought about it, she only ever remembered him having a glass with Andy, never on his own.

Andy followed him inside. It was so hot, and Athol had the car keys. Cindy had picked up a new purse that matched her floral dress and had forgotten to transfer her keys into it. So, within a few moments, she hurried back into the house and held the door ajar for Keisha to follow her. She sighed and let her eyes drift shut in the cool of the air conditioning. They stood there for several minutes, waiting for the men to return from the kitchen. But suddenly, Cindy heard raised voices echoing down the hallway.

She offered Keisha a startled look, then set her purse on the floor, and traveled in the direction of the kitchen, her heels clacking on the tiles.

"What's going on in here?" she asked, coming across Athol and Andy faced off against each other.

Neither of the men heard her, they were too busy yelling. Athol's fists were clenched at his sides. Andy waved his arms wildly overhead as he shouted.

Cindy stamped a foot. "Stop it!" But her voice didn't carry over the noise and they paid her no mind at all.

"I don't even like Scotch!" shouted Athol. It was the first thing either one of the men said that Cindy could decipher.

"What do you mean? Of course you do. We've always drunk it together."

"That's because you like it. I hate the stuff."

Andy shook his head and with a growl and threw his hands in the air. "So, I guess that's a symbol of our friendship right there. You pretended to care, while I was genuine. And now you don't even bother to carry your best friend's drink anymore! Some friend you are. Just gave up on me because of one little mishap."

Cindy's eyes narrowed and she pressed her hands to her hips. She really wanted to object to the *little mishap* suggestion, especially since he seemed to be referring to their decades-long marriage ending after an affair with his secretary. But she restrained herself since Athol looked as though his head was about to pop from his body. He seethed with anger and strode in a half-circle around Andy, then spun on his heel and strode back.

"Mishap? Mishap? That's what you call it? You self-centred, narcissistic…"

"Oh you're such a self-righteous prig! Always the angel. You never do anything wrong and I'm the bad guy who messes it up every single time."

"Well, if the shoe fits…" Athol laughed, but his eyes blazed.

"It's just whiskey," said Keisha, standing beside Cindy.

"Who cares?" But they didn't hear her either. She crossed her arms over her chest and lazed against the side of the kitchen table, watching with what looked like bored disinterest.

Cindy inhaled a deep breath. She was about to interrupt them when Andy spoke again.

"I've never been good enough for you. Perhaps we weren't friends after all. You saw me as a charity case, you were the perfect little doctor, and I was the shady finance guy. You never really cared about me."

She couldn't help feeling as though Andy had loved Athol more than he did her, since he'd never shown this much emotion over their marriage breakdown. But it didn't matter anymore since she'd forgiven him and put the past behind her. Athol, however, seemed to be holding the past very close to his chest. So close, in fact, that his neck was blotched with emotion and his face such a dark shade of red it was almost purple.

"Of course I cared about you, not that you deserved it. You were a selfish friend, just like you were a selfish husband. But I stood up for you, I told people you didn't mean it when you trampled all over them and their feelings. I said you were a good guy deep down when people woke up to your cruelty. But no more. I'm not defending you one more time. I've wasted too many years caring about the likes of you."

Cindy had no idea her husband was so passionate in his anger towards her ex. It was gratifying to see someone get the chance to take him down a peg or two, even if it couldn't be her. For the first time in her life, she saw that she finally had a husband who would stand his ground for her, who would defend her. He wouldn't back down to please other people, he wouldn't let her heart be trampled or push her feelings aside to pander to the crowd.

She wished she could throw her arms around Athol's

neck in that moment and kiss him on the lips. But they were now officially late to Sarah's dinner party, and getting later by the moment. She didn't know how they could show up late to Mick and Sarah's and pretend everything was all right, with the way things were going.

Andy stood in silence, his hands limp by his sides. "If that's how you really feel."

"It is."

"Then, I think Keisha and me will drive our own car to Sarah's." Andy turned and stalked away, with Keisha trotting after him on her impossibly high, red stilettos.

Athol and Cindy stayed behind in the kitchen. She claimed a chair at the round table and rested her chin in her hands.

"I guess you've got a bit of anger pent up there," she said.

He laughed and sat across from her before scrubbing his hands over his face. "I guess so. Sorry about that. He makes me so angry. I don't know what else to say about it."

"No need to apologise to me. I completely understand. He's self-centred and doesn't think about anyone else. But he's always been that way, and he's not going to change. The worst of it is, he doesn't see it in himself. So, he probably thinks you're being completely unfair. At least, that's what he used to say to me when I called him out on his selfishness."

"Why does he think I should buy him a one-hundred-dollar bottle of Scotch with everything that's happened? I don't like it, I never have. But I used to buy it for him. Now he thinks I'm being uncaring by not keeping it in stock."

"I guess he thought you'd forgive him and the two of you would go back to being good friends again, after the wedding was over."

Athol shook his head. "Well, if that's what he thought, he was living in a fantasy world."

"It's his favourite destination," replied Cindy, reaching out for Athol's hand, and squeezing it.

He smiled. "Thanks for being understanding. I was out of line."

"No, you weren't. This is our house, and he didn't ask if he could stay here. I still can't believe they expect us to put them up. This is how he was when we were married as well. He thinks I'm here to serve him. Whatever Andy wants, Cindy makes sure he gets it. That's how he's lived for so long, he doesn't see how wrong it is."

Athol stood behind Cindy and rubbed her shoulders, working out the tension that'd lodged there. "I won't let him treat you that way. If he's going to stay here, and I suppose we should do the right thing and let them stay since they're family, he's going to treat you with respect."

"I'm fine with that," replied Cindy, her eyes drifting shut as the massage helped ease her stress levels.

"Should we go?" He stepped away and reached out a hand towards her.

She took his hand. "We should. Although I have no idea how we'll make it through tonight. Or tomorrow."

Athol laughed. "At least we can sincerely say that life is never dull."

CHAPTER 16

SARAH

*T*here was so much to do, but she couldn't do any of it. Sarah sat in the armchair in the nursery feeding Leo. He'd been fussing for the past hour, and he was hungry. Everyone would be at the house soon for Christmas Eve dinner and she was sitting down, her fingers drumming a rhythm on the soft arm of the chair, waiting for him to finish feeding.

In her pocket, her mobile phone buzzed. She answered it without checking the screen. "Hello?"

"Hi, honey, it's Mick."

"Mick, where are you? It's getting late." She squeezed her eyes shut, as she did her best not to sound agitated. But the fact was, it was Christmas Eve, they were expecting the entire family any minute now and her husband had been at work all day long.

"I'm sorry, honey. I'm on my way now. The client had an utter meltdown this morning since we're so far behind schedule. Of course, we're not behind the schedule that I told him, but he had a completely different impression of how things would go in his head, so he lost the plot."

"That's so unfair. You belong with your family, instead you're working on his renovation to meet his impossible deadline. He should kiss the ground you walk on."

Mick laughed. "You're right. Anyway, I'm putting the truck into first, so I'd better get off the phone. I'll see you in half an hour."

She told him she loved him and hung up the phone then stared at the screen for a full minute as she measured her breathing — in, and out, in and out. There was no time to be enraged, angry, or tearful over it since she'd be entertaining guests soon. But she wanted to scream, cry, and punch someone — preferably her husband's client. How could he expect Mick to perform a miracle, then shout at him and make him late to Christmas Eve dinner at his own house? Of course, the client didn't think about how it would impact her, or that she had a two-month-old baby to care for and that she needed her husband at home with them. But it was still completely and utterly unfair, and she had to fight back the tears before they spilled out onto her cheeks.

It was ridiculous to be upset about something so trivial. There were people dying, homeless, separated from their families. She was crying over her husband coming home late to Christmas Eve dinner. She should be grateful he was so busy they could afford to live in a beautiful house by the beach. She sniffled and wiped her nose with a tissue. Time for an attitude adjustment. It was all going to be okay. In fact, she was excited to see the family. She loved it when her family got together, it was something she didn't take for granted any longer. Especially since her parents' divorce and Mum's recent illness.

Downstairs, there was a knock at the door. She shouted

for whoever it was to come in, then hoped as she heard the front door click open that it was Mum and Athol, as she'd imagined it would be, rather than a serial killer or a thief doing the rounds on the prowl for Christmas gifts to steal.

When Mum's smooth voice called up the stairs, "Hel-loooo!" Sarah breathed a sigh of relief.

"Upstairs in the nursery, Mum. I'll be down in a minute. Make yourselves at home."

A few seconds past and Mum burst into the nursery. "Hi sweetheart, how lovely to see you. You look wonderful."

Sarah smiled as Mum kissed her cheek. She finished feeding Leo then handed him to her mother to burp. "Here you go, Mum. He's all yours."

With a sigh, she tided the nursery. "I'm going to put him to bed, then I'll be able to focus on everything that's going on."

"Where's Mick?" asked Mum, patting Leo gently over her shoulder.

"At work."

"What? Still?"

"Yes, still. I mean, I knew he had to work, but it's six o'clock and he's still half an hour away. He's been working so hard to get this project finished before Christmas, that he's utterly exhausted. I can't blame him for being late since he's got this nightmare client to deal with. But still, it's a little frustrating. It's Leo's first Christmas and I feel like we're completely overwrought and not able to take any of it in. I wanted to relish it, to savour every moment. I had this picture-perfect idea of how it would go in my head — I thought we'd both read *The Night Before Christmas* together to Leo, then put him to bed and walk hand in hand down the stairs to have a drink on the back deck while the sun set behind the garden." She sighed and crossed her arms over her chest.

LILLY MIRREN

Mum offered her a sympathetic smile as she changed Leo's nappy. "Oh sweetheart, that's a lovely idea, even if it is a little bit idealistic."

"I didn't think of myself as idealistic before now."

"Well, everyone is idealistic when they have their first baby. But having babies is the busiest time of your entire life. Yes, you want to make sure you pause every now and then to soak it all in. But most of the time you'll be tired, run off your feet, and doing your very best to manage your career and pay the bills — and it happens all at once, I'm afraid. You have to find joy in the midst of the fatigue and busyness. Don't wait for the perfect moments, enjoy the moments you have." She snapped the buttons on Leo's suit back together, gave him a kiss and handed him to Sarah. "Here you go, one freshly changed and burped baby, ready for bed."

Sarah smiled and took Leo into her arms. "Thanks, Mum. I don't know what I'd do without you sometimes."

"I'm glad to be able to help, sweetheart. I never had anyone to help me, and I don't want that for you."

"You were still a great mother," replied Sarah, as she lay Leo in his cot. "I don't know how you managed it."

"I didn't always manage it well. But I tried to focus on the things that mattered — like loving you, kisses, and cuddles. Plus plenty of good food for you to eat. Those are the things that make an impact, I think. I didn't often have time to play, but I did make an effort to listen when you had something you wanted to tell me."

"I remember you always being available," replied Sarah. "Thanks Mum. Are you feeling any better today?"

Mum offered a wan smile. "Better and better every day. This medication is doing wonders."

Sarah wasn't sure if Mum was being entirely honest. But she hoped so. She was scared to death of anything happening to her mother. She'd taken her for granted for so long. Now

142

that she'd realised how important her mother was to her happiness, it frightened her to think of something going wrong.

She linked her arm through Mum's, and they walked down the stairs together. Sarah carried the baby monitor with her and set it on the kitchen bench. She greeted Dad, Keisha, and Athol who all seemed to be scattered across the kitchen, dining room, and living room. Athol sat on his own in the living room, one leg crossed over the other, reading a book. Not exactly the type of thing she expected him to be doing at a dinner party, but she wasn't one to judge, and she wasn't in the frame of mind to say something witty.

Instead she said, "Merry Christmas everyone. Now, who would like a drink?"

* * *

An hour later, everyone had arrived, and the food Mum brought was displayed on the table on the outside deck, along with a few appetisers Sarah had pulled from the freezer and thawed in the oven. Christmas music played through the sound system, soft lilting melodies from famous jazz musicians that she and Mick had selected. Mick had emerged from the shower a few minutes earlier, freshly washed and smelling infinitely better than he had when he got home.

Adele brought a bottle of wine and a bunch of fresh flowers, and Sarah was in the process of adding water to a vase when the delivery of Chinese food she'd ordered arrived. Usually she loved to cook and would've revelled in putting together a menu for the evening. But she'd made a lemon meringue pie for dessert and had run out of time to do anything else. The only restaurant in town doing deliveries for Christmas Eve was the Chinese Garden, and so she'd ordered Beef and Black bean, Cashew Chicken, Dumplings, fried rice, and Seafood with Oyster Sauce.

She shoved the flowers into the vase and hurried to answer the front door. She grabbed Mick by the arm on her way and he trotted after her saying, "Ouch, why are you pinching me?"

"Sorry, I need help with the food," she whispered. "And I know the family is not going to be happy, since we have our traditional dishes for Christmas Eve every year and this isn't it. But I couldn't manage it, so they're going to have to get over it."

Mick rubbed his arm, paid the delivery man, and took the bags. "Fine, but perhaps you could leave me some skin next time."

She offered him a forced smile. "I'm doing my best to hold it all together. So, I'm sorry if I pinched you. But have you noticed that Athol isn't talking to anyone? Dad and Keisha have almost buried themselves in the drinks cart, and Mum is using that high-pitched voice that means she's on the verge of shouting? It's really only a matter of time until everything falls apart. So we have to feed these people and get them out of our house, so I can get some sleep."

"Merry Christmas to all," said Mick, one eyebrow arched. "And to all…"

Her nostrils flared. "Don't start with me."

He laughed. "You have *got* to calm down."

"I'm cool as a cucumber."

"Okay, great. Why don't I pour you a drink, and I'll set up the rest of the food outside? You can relax."

"You've been on your feet working all day," she argued, marching back down the hallway, carrying a brown paper bag full of Chinese takeaway containers.

Ahead of her, Mick set his bag on the kitchen bench and headed for the drinks cart. "I really don't mind, honey. Here you go, I'll make you a lemon lime and bitters in this fancy Christmas glass." He handed her a drink with ice floating on top. "Now, you go and sit outside, enjoy yourself, and I'll bring the food out to the table."

"The serving dishes are behind you," she said.

He waved her away. "I know, I'm on top of it. I promise."

Sarah wandered out to the back deck, suddenly unsure of what to do. She'd been running around waiting on people, tidying, washing dishes, and preparing trays of appetisers and finger foods for the past hour. She'd spent the day cleaning, taking care of Leo, and answering emails. Now, she found herself with nothing to do but to sit and sip her drink.

She found a chair beside Adele, and crossed one leg over the other, smoothing out her green silk dress with her free hand.

"You look beautiful," said Adele, with a smile.

"You do too. I love the gold skirt. I could never get away with that."

Adele laughed. "Of course you could."

"How are things at the cafe?"

"Oh, fine, I think. We're shut tonight and tomorrow, thank goodness. It's been absolutely crazy all week. So many tourists are in town. We've been run off our feet. I'm glad to have a break, even if it is only a brief one."

"I bet," replied Sarah.

"And what about you? How's the book going?"

Sarah took a sip of her drink, as her stomach churned. Even thinking about her book gave her indigestion. "It's going well, I suppose. The preorders are surpassing their expectations. So that's good. Although Pauline wants me to start my book tour right after Christmas."

"Book tour?" asked Adele, her brow furrowed. "What would that involve?"

"Travelling all over the country to bookstores, libraries,

and so on, to sign books and read excerpts for fans. But I don't really have any fans, since this is my first book. So, who knows if anyone will even show up?"

"When does the book release?"

"The first of January." Sarah gulped another mouthful of gin and tonic.

"What do you think about it all?"

Sarah hesitated. "I don't know what to think. Of course, since I used to be an editor, I understand how it all works. I know what's expected of me. But still, Leo is only two months old. I'm not sure how well I can manage a book tour with a baby. And then, what about Mick? Do we simply leave him behind? He's so busy with work at the moment, he can't take any time off."

Adele wrapped an arm around Sarah's shoulders. "Sounds complicated."

"It is." She combed fingers through her straight brown hair, letting it settle over her shoulders. Twinkle lights sparkled around the railing that lined the deck. The murmur of conversation filled the air, as guests milled about. The garden glowed with light from several solar-powered lanterns scattered throughout the rose bushes.

"I'm sure you'll figure it out."

"I'm considering asking to postpone it. For a little while, at least. And maybe we could break it up into smaller portions, travel for a few days, then take a break, and so on." She shrugged. "It might work better than one big tour."

"That sounds infinitely more achievable." Adele kissed her cheek. "You're amazing, do you know that? Such an inspiration to me."

Sarah's face flushed with warmth. "Really?"

"Absolutely, I don't know how you do it, but you always manage to achieve whatever you set out to. And you do it all with such grace." Adele smiled. "It's genuinely disgusting." Her eyes crossed and she poked out her tongue.

Sarah laughed. "Oh shut up." She playfully slapped Adele's shoulder, then hugged her with her free arm. "You're the inspirational one. I still can't believe you left home at eighteen to train to become a pilot. You have no fear, at all."

"I have fears, I try not to listen to them."

"Well, it's very impressive."

"Thanks, big sis."

Mick finished adding the final dish to the table, then clapped his hands together to call everyone to attention. "Good evening, all! Thank you so much for coming tonight. Sarah and I feel very honoured to have you all here with us in our new home, for our first Christmas together as a family of three. Leo is of course upstairs sleeping soundly through the entire dinner party." There were a few chuckles throughout the group. "But he'd want me to thank you all for coming. The food is ready, so please grab a plate. Let's say grace."

He prayed and the family lined up beside the table to pile their plates high with food. Sarah heard a few mumbled complaints about the Chinese food. Ethan wondered where the potato salad was. Dad questioned Mum about the absence of ham. But everyone took a slice of Mum's homemade bread with a small square of lasagna. Sarah was grateful her mother had managed to throw them together without much notice. At last, each guest had a full plate and had found somewhere to sit, or perch, in the dining room, living room or on the porch.

Diana had come along with Emily and Ethan. Dad and Keisha sat with them in the dining room, while the rest of the family, as well as a few family friends, found spaces elsewhere to sit. Sarah sat beside Mick on a bench seat on the deck and balanced her plate of food on her lap.

Mum and Athol were nearby on another bench seat.

"The lasagna is amazing, Mum," said Sarah, around a mouthful.

Mum smiled. "Glad to hear it."

"Thanks for bringing so much food."

"You're welcome."

"The Chinese food is a great touch," said Athol, waving his fork at the table. "I love it. The Chinese Garden has the best fried rice."

"Thanks, Athol. I know it's not our traditional offering, but I couldn't face anymore cooking or baking right now."

"That's understandable," he replied.

Ethan was serving himself a second helping of lasagna. "Come on Sarah, you've got more energy than anyone else I know. Surely, you could've thrown a ham in the oven. You know how much I love the Christmas ham Mum does every year."

Sarah bit back the first retort that sprung to mind. "You'll understand when you have a newborn."

He laughed, eyes twinkling. "How hard could it be? He's so tiny, and he's asleep every time I come over here."

Dad sidled through the back door and found a space beside Ethan to refill his plate. "What are we talking about?"

"I asked Sarah why there was no ham, and she said it was too much of a hassle."

Irritation buzzed in Sarah's gut. "That's not exactly what I said, Ethan. I told you I couldn't manage it because I have too much going on right now."

"There'll be ham tomorrow Ethan. And babies are harder than you think they'll be," piped up Mum, before popping a dumpling into her mouth.

"Come on, he's so tiny. And I don't think I've seen him cry once. All he does is smile and sleep." Ethan winked.

Sarah knew he was purposely irritating her by baiting her

with his words. He'd done it their entire lives. He'd been her annoying younger brother who went out of his way to wind her up. But she wasn't going to fall for it this time.

"It's true, he's adorable," replied Dad. "You really got a good one there, Sarah. I don't think you can complain about him."

"I'm not complaining," she replied, feeling her temperature rise. "But he takes up a lot of my time."

"As well he should," responded Dad. "Too many people these days think babies should simply slot into their busy lives, so they can keep on doing all the things they were doing before. Babies should take up most of your time. That's what having a family is like."

Sarah bit down on her tongue. She wasn't about to point out how much of her own childhood her father had missed because he was off cavorting with his mistress or playing golf with his buddies. It was Christmas and she wouldn't react to his provocation. Not this time.

"We know what having a family is like," said Mick. His voice was cold. "But none of you, apart from Cindy and Athol, have bothered to ask Sarah if she needed help tonight. You all expect her to wait on you, and that's fine. But please don't criticise or act like she's being overly sensitive, when she tells you she's struggling. I haven't been here for her this week like I should've been, and I can see the strain it's taking on her. So, let's all be a little bit more thoughtful and supportive, please."

Sarah gaped at her husband. Somehow, in a few sentences, he'd succinctly and politely expressed exactly how she was feeling. He'd put her family in their place without disrespecting them or raising his voice. Usually, she'd end up shouting at them and storming out of the room to cry alone in a corner somewhere. But he was calm, collected, and completely at ease with the direction the conversation had taken, even as his firm words left no room for misunder-standing.

There was an uneasy silence as everyone either stared at their plate or ate quietly. Then, Dad cleared his throat.

"Uh, yes well of course. Thank you for everything you do, Sarah. We don't take you for granted."

"Thanks Dad, I appreciate it."

"Yeah, love you Sassy-Pants." Ethan grinned, then popped a forkful of lasagna into his mouth.

When Ethan and Dad had headed back inside, Sarah breathed a sigh of relief. "Thank you," she whispered to Mick. He nodded in response, too busy eating to say anything more.

After dinner, they all sat around the living room and played a game of charades while they sipped eggnog spiked with spiced rum. They ended the night laughing and chatting, with no tension in the air or anything unspoken between them. At least it seemed that way to Sarah. Whatever had gone on between Mum, Athol, Dad and Keisha, seemed to have blown over, and she was grateful. She hoped they could all share Christmas Day together tomorrow without any fights or conflict.

When everyone else had left, she found Adele in the kitchen putting away clean dishes in the cupboards.

"Whatever is left to do, we can finish tomorrow," said Sarah with yawn. "Leo will be up in two hours. I've got to get some sleep."

"What do you think of me sleeping over tonight?" said Adele, as she threw a dishtowel over her shoulder and leaned against the bench.

"You want to sleep in your old room?"

"If that's okay with you. Then, I can help you with Leo and let you get some sleep."

"That would be amazing," replied Sarah, eyes widening.

"There's milk in the fridge, all you have to do is heat it up. I have to get up with him in two hours, but maybe you could do the early morning feed?"

"I'd be happy to. His room is right next to mine, so I should hear him pretty clearly when he wakes up."

"Wow, that would be so wonderful. That's the best Christmas gift you could give me."

"Say, your hubby was pretty wonderful tonight," said Adele with a wink. "So confident and firm. The way he stood up for you was hot."

"Was it?" Sarah laughed. "I guess you're right. He's a keeper."

"Definitely. I love that he has your back like that. Sometimes Dad and Ethan can be a bit much, especially when they gang up like that. Usually, you get so upset with them. But he stepped in, and they really listened to him and backed off."

"It was pretty great," admitted Sarah. "It's nice to have a partner in life."

"I hope I can find someone like that one day."

"You will," replied Sarah, giving Adele a hug. She yawned so wide it seemed her face might split in two. "I've got to get to bed. I'll see you in the morning."

As she padded up the stairs, she considered Adele's words. She was so grateful for Mick. Sometimes, she almost had to pinch herself to remember that he was her husband, and that they'd vowed to spend the rest of their lives together. She couldn't imagine her life without him now, and with Leo as part of their family, their lives were so much fuller than they'd been before. She didn't want to be someone who complained about getting everything she'd dreamed of. Tomorrow was a new day and she'd start it with gratitude — for her husband, her child, and a family who cared, even if they could be irritating and entitled at times.

CHAPTER 17

25TH DECEMBER

ADELE

*H*er eyes blinked open, and she lay in the stillness of her childhood bedroom staring at the wall for several seconds in silence. What had woken her? The cacophony of birdcalls that accompanied every dawn drifted through the open window. Overhead, a ceiling fan spun slowly, making a soft whirring noise and a click with every rotation.

There it was again. A brief, muffled cry. Adele sat up with a yawn and rubbed her eyes. She slipped into her blue satin dressing gown and tiptoed down the hall a short way to Leo's bedroom. He lay on his back, staring straight up at the ceiling. Then his face crumpled and he let out another cry, louder this time, and he seemed to have no intention of stopping.

"Hey there baby boy," she whispered, scooping him up and holding him against her chest. "Merry Christmas. It's your first Christmas ever and I'm the lucky one who gets to wake up with you and tell you all about Santa Claus."

She bounced a little with each step, as she walked him to the change table. The crying stopped and he seemed to be wondering who it was that'd come into his bedroom. He was expecting Sarah at this time of day, but instead he'd gotten Auntie Adele, and she couldn't help grinning at him when she lay him on the change table and noticed his wide, blue eyes were fixed on her face.

"Surprise!" she whispered, doing a peek-a-boo with her hands. "I bet you weren't expecting to see me, huh?"

His gaze didn't leave her face, his eyes tracking her movements as she changed his nappy.

"I'm your Auntie Adele. Adele, can you say that? Not yet? Well, if you said it now, you'd give me a fright and you'd be a complete prodigy. But still, I'm going to tell you my name over and over, since I want it to be the first word you ever say. Adele, Adele. Your mum will be so furious if you say Adele before you say mum. It'll be absolutely priceless." She laughed softly and lifted the freshly changed baby up to her chest then kissed his forehead. The scent of his almost bald head gave her a rush of delight, and she giggled. "Ah fresh baby smell, it's the best. Come on, Leo, let's go and find you some milk."

In the kitchen, she set Leo in his bouncer while she heated the bottle of milk she found in the fridge. She warmed up the espresso machine on the bench, brewed herself a cup of coffee, and put it in a travel mug so it wouldn't spill. Then, she and Leo sat in the armchair in the living room. He drank milk. She sipped her coffee, leaning as far away from him as she could manage just in case a drop escaped. She told him all about Santa Claus and how he'd come to the house the night before to leave Leo a gift. His little eyes stayed fixed on her face as he sucked his bottle and listened intently to her story.

Finally, she flicked on the television and watched a sunrise Christmas service, with the volume almost entirely muted. Whenever a carol came on, she sang along to it in a hushed voice, watching for Leo's reaction. He seemed to enjoy it, so she kept it up until the service ended and he was finished with his bottle. Then she put Leo back in his bouncer and rocked him gently with one foot while she read a book from Sarah's bookshelf.

When Mick padded into the room in his pyjamas, hair tousled, he waved good morning without saying a word, and headed for the espresso machine. It soon whirred to life, and he fixed himself a cup of coffee.

"Want another cup?" he rasped.

"No thanks, I'm good."

He sat across from her, after kissing Leo on the head. Then he sighed as he settled down into the couch.

"Tired?" she asked.

"Hmmm," he replied. "Merry Christmas."

"Back at ya."

He smiled. "Thanks for getting up with Leo. It was nice to sleep in a little past five a.m."

"You're welcome. He's been completely adorable the whole time." She reached out and tickled his toes. He really was the cutest baby who ever lived, and she wasn't being biased. He had wide blue eyes and a perfectly round head with a tiny tuft of blonde hair. His cheeks were chubby and pink, and his small fists pumped randomly as he studied his surroundings from the bouncer.

"I know Sarah is happy to get some extra rest. She hasn't been sleeping very well."

"I'm glad to be able to help."

"You hungry?" he asked.

Her stomach clenched in response. Whenever she woke early, she was always famished for some reason. "I'm starved."

"Great, I'm going to make a big breakfast and we can eat until we burst."

She laughed. "Sounds perfect. I'll help you. We can bring the bouncer with us."

She carried Leo in his bouncer over to the dining room and set him on the table where they could see him. Then she set about making scrambled eggs, bacon, and toast, while Mick mixed a batch of pancakes, and warmed some berries in a saucepan.

Delicious aromas filled the kitchen, and the sizzling of bacon and pancakes on the griddle brought Sarah sleepily down the stairs.

"It smells amazing in here," she said, slumping onto a chair and giving Leo a kiss in the middle of his tummy. "Wow you were quiet this morning."

"He's been such a sweetheart. We had a lot of fun together."

"He usually cries so much more." Sarah yawned again. "It must've been Auntie Adele's special touch."

Adele laughed. "He loves me more, that's all."

"Of course he does," replied Sarah, kissing his cheek, and using a baby voice. "Who wouldn't love Auntie Adele?"

Sarah wandered into the kitchen and stole a piece of bacon. Adele playfully slapped at her hand, and Sarah grinned in response while she ate it in two bites before making herself a cup of coffee.

"I'm not complaining at all, but who is all this food for? There's only three of us here, you know." She sipped her coffee and perched on a barstool at the bench.

"We're famished," said Mick, giving Sarah a wink. "I

figure we can all eat until we're completely stuffed, then lay around the Christmas tree like beached whales while we open gifts. We don't have to be at your Mum and Athol's until eleven."

"I think that's a great plan," said Adele.

Sarah concurred, so they all joked and chatted as Sarah watched Adele and Mick make breakfast for the three of them. Just as they were about to sit down to eat, the front door opened and there were voices in the hall.

Sarah's brow furrowed as she bit into another piece of bacon. "Who is that?"

Adele frowned. "I have no idea." She hurried to the hallway and peered down it. Mum, Athol, Dad, and Keisha were all making their way towards the kitchen, chattering and laughing, laden down with armfuls of wrapped Christmas gifts.

They burst into the kitchen, all noise and conversation, giggling and celebrations. Each was still dressed in their pyjamas and robes and carried their gifts to lay beneath the Christmas tree in the living room before returning to the kitchen.

"What's going on?" asked Sarah, cinching the tie on her robe more tightly around her thin waist.

"We thought we'd surprise you," replied Mum.

Dad gave Sarah a wink. "Hope you don't mind, Chick-adee. We were all sitting around at your Mum and Athol's place, and we decided what we really wanted to do was come over here and see Leo. And the rest of you, of course. All us old fogeys hanging around a Christmas tree together drinking spiced eggnog isn't quite the same thing as having our kids gathered around us. Right Cindy?"

Mum nodded, clearly more giddy than usual. "Yes, that's right. Besides, your dad and Athol have something they want to tell you all."

Adele spooned the scrambled eggs into a large bowl and set them beside the plate of bacon and buttered toast. "Go ahead, Dad." She couldn't imagine what kind of announcement they were about to make, but by the look on her father's face it had something to do with his indiscretions. He always went red-faced whenever he had to admit culpability for something.

Just then, the front door opened again, and within moments, Ethan, Emily, and Diana had joined them. Ethan's eyes widened in surprise at the sight of the full kitchen and dining room.

"So this is where everyone's congregated," he said with a laugh.

"Come on in," replied Sarah. "Everyone's here, you might as well join us."

"We decided it was too quiet over at the Manor this morning. The staff has it all under control. So we thought we'd come and see what you were doing," said Emily, her cheeks flushing pink.

Diana gave Cindy a hug. "And I wanted to see my friends."

"Well, you're very welcome," replied Mick.

"Yes, you are." Cindy sniffled. "Oh, I'm so happy everyone's here."

"Dad was about to tell us all something," added Adele.

"Oh yeah? What's going on, Dad?" asked Ethan, as he slid onto a bar stool.

Dad cleared his throat. "Thanks, Cindy, for that introduction. First of all, I'm so grateful for all of you. This is a special day, and who better to share it with than each other. It's been a long couple of years and to me it seems like we've come out the other end of something. The air is lighter, the sun is brighter, and we're ready to move forward. In light of that, it's not a big deal, but I wanted to apologise. Athol and I had a bit of a row last night before we came over here, and I was in a foul mood. I'm afraid to say my temper may have ruined your lovely evening, Sarah and Mick. I felt bad about it after we got back to Cindy and Athol's, and so the four of us sat down together and hashed things out. We forgave each other, and we've all decided to move on and put the past behind us."

"That's right," added Athol, with a wide smile. He wrapped an arm around Dad's shoulders. "Your father and I have been good friends for too many decades to give up on it now. We've had our differences and our fights, but in the end, we'll always be in each other's lives. So, we're burying the hatchet, so to speak, and we're going to try to be on better behaviour today."

A lump grew in Adele's throat as the two men spoke. She hadn't thought a reconciliation between the two of them was possible. And even after everything Dad had done, she'd always had a soft spot for him. She hated to see him in pain. And she knew how much losing Athol's friendship had hurt him.

She hugged her father and buried her face in his shoulder. "I'm so glad, Dad. I know what Athol means to you. And it's not good for any of us to hold a grudge."

She embraced Athol as well. "Thank you, Athol. It's a Christmas miracle." She laughed. "Or something like that, anyway."

Cindy wiped her eyes with a tissue. "No, honey, you're right. It is something of a miracle. And I for one am glad to see it. What's done is done, and there's no use rehashing the past all the time. Besides, no matter what your father has done, he introduced me to Athol, who has brought me so much joy. So, I have to thank him for that."

"We're all happy for you," added Mick, in his booming voice. "And to celebrate, there's pancakes with yoghurt and berries, plus scrambled eggs, bacon, and toast for everyone!"

"I'll make coffees," added Adele. "I've become something of an expert at it."

She manned the coffee machine and took people's orders, while Mick ushered everyone to the table where he placed the platters of food, plates, and forks. She smiled as she worked, grateful to see that Sarah was happier as well after a good night's rest. With the tension released between Mum, Dad, Athol, and Keisha, the group gathered around the table to share happy conversations, delicious food, and hearty laughter. Everyone *oohed* and *aahed* over Leo, who'd been moved to lay on a play mat on the floor by the back door. Oscar rested just outside the door snoozing, only lifting his black head every now and then to thump his tail on the timber floor.

After breakfast, they gathered around the Christmas tree in their pjs, nursing cups of coffee and tea, and sat on couches, armchairs, or the floor to open gifts. Adele felt as though she might burst with joy. She couldn't remember a Christmas morning as happy as this one.

CHAPTER 18

CARLOS

*S*weat trickled down his back and down the sides of his face. It was hot, but he was nervous too. The nervous tension made him hotter than ever as Carlos stood beside Tito on the threshold to the Miller house. He raised a fist and knocked on the door. Inside there were voices raised in conversation and laughter. Music drifted out to greet them — a jaunty Christmas carol. The scent of freshly baked bread was intoxicating. But no one answered the door.

"Well, this is awkward," he said.

Tito shrugged. "Try again."

He knocked again, and this time someone shouted "Come in" from inside the house.

Carlos opened the door and followed Tito into the house. The cool air enveloped them, driving away the heat. A sprig of mistletoe hung over them in the hallway. There was a photograph above a hall table of Adele's entire family grin-

161

ning and laughing in black and white. Then, the hallway opened out into a small living room with an attached kitchen and dining area. There were people everywhere. People he didn't know or recognise. He felt so completely out of place.

"It's strange to be barging in on some other family's Christmas Day," he muttered under his breath.

"Eh?" said Tito.

Carlos simply shook his head. "Nothing."

"Where is Adele?" asked Tito.

Before Carlos could respond, a woman approached them. She had greyish-blonde hair in a fluffy bob and wore a red silk top over a pair of jeans. "You must be Carlos and Samuel," she said. "Come on in, you're very welcome in my home. I'm Cindy Miller, and that over there is my husband Athol."

She pointed to an older gentleman with grey hair who stood in a corner of the kitchen pouring ginger ale into a punch bowl. He offered them a wave and a smile.

"It's nice to meet you," said Carlos.

"We're so glad you could come and spend some time with us today. I'll find Adele for you, since I've got an emergency with a batch of muffins I have to attend to."

Carlos and Samuel placed gifts they'd brought beneath the small Christmas tree in the living room. Carlos set a bag of drinks on the bench. He wasn't sure what else he should do. Everyone around them was busy, engaged in conversation, or hurrying here or there. A woman held a small baby and crooned a Christmas song while rocking the child in her arms. Adele was outside, and she hurried in as soon as Cindy caught her attention. She embraced Samuel, then kissed Carlos's cheek. He was surprised by how comfortable and happy he felt in her presence. They barely knew each other, yet it was as if she was an old friend, someone he'd known for years.

"Hi," she said.

"Hi," he replied.

They stood looking at each other while Carlos's cheeks flamed.

"I'm going to introduce myself to Athol," said Tito with a shake of his head. "You kids have fun."

Carlos pushed his hands into the pockets of his shorts. "I found a job," he said. "They called me yesterday."

"Oh wow, that's great. Where is it?"

"That psychologist's office where we first met. I'm going to intern there and work as a casual receptionist."

"That's perfect for you," exclaimed Adele.

"Yeah, I'm pretty happy about it. And now I can pay my rent. So, that's a bonus."

She laughed. "I know what you mean. Paying rent is definitely a good thing. Hey, it's loud in here, I can barely hear you with all the noise. Do you want to take a walk?"

"I'd love to. But I'd really like to get to know your family better too."

She smiled and her eyes glistened. "Good to know."

They walked together down the hallway. Adele stopped at the hall table and picked up a small purse.

"I'll get my phone and we can leave. I'm sure no one will notice. They're all busy making lunch and talking about who knows what. Ah, here it is." She tugged her phone free of the purse and held it aloft in triumph.

Carlos glanced up and noticed the sprig of mistletoe was directly overhead. Adele's gaze followed his, up to where the green leaves tied with red ribbon hung neat and high from the ceiling on a short piece of string.

"Mistletoe," she said.

He smiled. "I guess that means…"

"We have to kiss. It's tradition, and you can't argue with tradition." She grinned.

"Well, since it's tradition." Carlos cupped her cheeks with his hands and leaned down to press his lips against hers. Her skin was soft, her lips warm and inviting. He didn't want to pull away, didn't want to stop. Their kiss set a spark of life deep within his soul that flickered into flame. It wound its way up through his body like a bolt of energy that brought every part of him to life.

When the kiss finally ended, his eyes were still shut as he took a step back. Slowly, they blinked open, and it seemed the world was a different place to the one he'd lived in before. Before that kiss.

"Wow," said Adele, echoing his thoughts.

"Yeah."

"That was unexpected." She laughed. "Let's go." She reached for his hand and slipped hers into it. Then, she pulled him through the front door. They ran down the street together hand-in-hand. It was exhilarating. He couldn't remember a time he'd felt so alive. His hand fairly vibrated at her touch. The sun seared his scalp, and the breeze from the ocean was heady with the scent of flowers and fresh cut grass. They reached the beach within a few minutes and slowed their pace to stroll, lazy and hot, along the water's edge.

He talked about his family, his mother and Yaya. The pain he and Tito had lived in for so long, and how they finally felt as though they were emerging from it. She told him more about her past, her career, and the cafe.

"Do you think you'll stay here in the Cove?" asked Carlos when Adele finished speaking.

"I don't know. What about you?"

"I hope so," he said. "It's definitely growing on me. I mean, where else in the world can you find a beach like this?" He gestured, a sweeping wave that took in the beach, the gentle waves, azure waters that sparkled like jewels, and the black rocks that rose like the backs of a herd of beasts at both ends of the beach.

"It's beautiful here, I know. I took it for granted until I traveled. I had the chance to fly to places all over Australia and Asia. There is a lot of beauty out there, but nothing like this — with such kind people, my family, the cafe. Everything and everyone I care about is here. And even though all I wanted to do a few years ago was to get away from it all and forge my own path in life, now I can't imagine living anywhere else."

"I can see why you love it. Tito wants to stay, to live out the rest of his days here by the beach. It's been a lifelong dream of his. And so, I'll stay here while I can. I have to be close to him, but I like the idea of settling down somewhere as well. Besides, it's close to the university and if I need to go to Brisbane for work, it's not far either."

She stopped walking and stood in front of him, winding her fingers through his. With both hands connected, they stared at each other. A half smile played around the corners of her mouth.

"And maybe you'll stay here for me as well," she said.

"Maybe," he replied, with a grin.

He pulled a small package out of his pocket and handed it to her. It'd been hard to make a decision over what to buy her for Christmas. He'd gone back and forth for days, visiting the jewellers repeatedly to stare at the items in the velvet-clothed cases.

"What is this?" she asked.

"You'll have to open it to find out. Merry Christmas."

"Wow, thank you. I left your gift back at the house."

He grinned. "Come on, open it."

She tore open the paper and found the square black box

inside. She flicked open the lid and gaped. A gold necklace with a small gold circle looped around the chain stared back at her, glinting beneath the sunlight.

"You got me a necklace?"

"It's not much," he said. "But it reminded me of you."

He helped her put it on, slipping it around her neck as she lifted her hair from her shoulders.

"Thank you," she said, fingering it gently. "I love it. I can't believe you got me a necklace. That's so beautiful. I only got you a book about planes. Now I feel bad."

He laughed. "I love planes."

She reached for him then, standing on her tiptoes to kiss him. She wove one arm around his neck, pulling him down to her to deepen the kiss. Behind them the waves crashed to shore, and in moments the cool, bubbling water submerged their feet and ankles. Then with a rush it was gone.

"We should get back," she said, finally, with their foreheads pressed together.

Her eyes were blue and wide. He could get lost in their depths if she let him.

"We should," he agreed without moving.

"They'll notice we're gone soon if they haven't already. And I promised Sarah I'd refill the salsa and chips."

He smiled. "Then we should go and do that. Besides, I haven't met all of your family yet. I'd like to."

"Yeah?"

"Definitely," he said. "And Tito is probably telling all kinds of embarrassing stories about me that I should put a stop to."

She laughed. He wanted to hear that laugh forever. It lit him up and made him smile.

"I want to hear those embarrassing stories."

"I'm sure Tito will oblige."

"Okay, then we should get going."

With a sigh, they agreed and finally drew apart.

Then, hand-in-hand, they continued along the beach. Carlos couldn't believe how quickly the day had changed. He no longer felt like an awkward stranger at someone else's celebration. His heart thudded and a joy he didn't recognise bubbled up within him, making his head feel light.

CHAPTER 19

CINDY

"You're hopeless at washing the dishes," admonished Cindy, slapping Andy's hand away from the dishwasher. "Leave it, I'll do it. As usual." She rolled her eyes as laughing, Andy backed out of the kitchen with his hands raised in surrender.

"Then, I'm out of here. You can deal with her, Athol, she's all yours now. No longer my problem."

"Don't remind me," murmured Athol, his nose buried in a newspaper at the kitchen table.

"Hey!" objected Cindy.

"Just joking, sweetheart," added Athol, winking at her over the paper.

A song came onto the radio about a long-lost love. It irritated her. Her former love was in her living room with a smug grin on his face after having wormed his way out of doing the dishes once again. Christmas was over. Carols no longer played on any of the stations. All the classic Christmas movies were finished for the year. Soon she'd have to take down the decorations and put away all the gifts. Her favourite time of year was over, again.

Andy slumped into an armchair and flicked on the television. He cranked up the volume so that it drowned out the radio. Her frown lines deepened, and she set about restocking the dishwasher after Andy's failed attempt. He really was horrible at doing any kind of housework. Although, even after all these years, she still wasn't sure if he did that intentionally or if he was completely oblivious to how incompetently he tackled household chores. The difference was that now, she didn't care. As he'd so eloquently put it, they were no longer each other's problem.

This year, things hadn't gone to plan — she couldn't travel when she wanted, her health had been through some ups and downs, but in the end, she spent the holiday with the people she loved most. That's what mattered.

Keisha wandered into the kitchen and set her mobile on the bench with a sigh. "Well, that was the pest control company. Our house is cleared for us to return." Her almond-shaped eyes narrowed. "Although I'm not sure I believe them or trust that they're telling me the truth. They've sprayed the entire place with poison, I don't know if I'll ever want to go back there. I'm sure they don't care if I die. Perhaps we should stay here a little longer." She examined a long, red fingernail closely, her brow furrowing with concentration.

Cindy wiped her hands dry on a tea towel and hurried to comfort her. "No, don't say that. They definitely wouldn't let you go home unless it was completely safe to do so. Right Athol?" She peered over her shoulder at Athol who glanced up with the kind of expression on his face that suggested he'd only half heard whatever it was she'd addressed to him.

"Uh, yes, of course."

"See, Athol's a doctor, he'd never advise you to go into a dangerous situation. You can trust the pest company, and you can trust Athol. Your home is perfectly safe." She pressed a hand to Keisha's back, gently directing her out of the kitchen and towards the staircase which led to the guest room where her and Andy's things were strewn about over the floor, the bed, a chair and in the bathroom. "And I'm sure the two of you are dying to get back to your own space. I know how hard it is to stay with other people over the holidays."

"It *is* tiring," admitted Keisha, moving up the stairs with reluctance.

"Of course it is. You pack up your things and I'll send a nice little lunch package home with you, with all the tasty Christmas leftovers in it."

"Turkey?" asked Keisha, her glistening red lips pouting.

"Yes, turkey with stuffing of course. There's potato salad, ham, and even a little bit of breakfast casserole from this morning."

"Hmmm...I suppose we *should* get going. I could take a nap this afternoon. All this rushing around, so many people. I don't know how you manage it, Cindy, without totally losing your mind. It's been bedlam around here."

Cindy shook her head. "It's a mystery. I suppose I'm simply used to it."

After watching Keisha pick her way up the staircase, she returned to the kitchen with a smile on her face. Andy flicked off the television, declaring there was nothing good on, and he might as well stare at the wall as watch anything on that tiny little screen.

"Why don't you lash out for a big screen, Athol? A rich

doctor like you. Surely you can afford anything you like. I don't understand why you wouldn't want a big screen." Andy pressed his hands to his hips, glaring at the offending screen as though doing so would spontaneously enlarge it.

Athol ignored him, other than a silent shake of his head behind the newspaper.

As she rinsed out a dish and stacked it in the dishwasher, Cindy whistled along to the music on the radio. Andy's little tirade didn't bother her one bit. He could rant all day long about television screens, the music on the radio, the scratchy sheets, or her cooking. It made no difference because he was leaving. She'd finally have her house back to herself. She and Athol would be alone again. Alone never sounded so good.

"What are you so happy about?" asked Andy, biting into a croissant with cheese and ham left over from breakfast. Crumbs dropped to the bench and the floor all around him.

She pulled a plate from the cupboard and handed it to him with a cluck of the tongue. "Even your crumbs aren't going to upset me, Flannigan."

He grinned. "You used to be a Flannigan."

Her smile widened. "Not anymore, baby."

"You're in a very good mood," he reiterated.

"And you're heading home," she replied. "Keisha heard from the pest company, you've got the all clear. She's upstairs packing right now."

Andy's grin faded. He crossed his arms over his chest. "I know you didn't want us around, Cindy. But I thought we'd gotten past that. All I want for us is to be friends. You and I were family for so long, I don't know how to do this whole thing without you. And Athol's been my best friend for as long as I can remember." He shook his head. "I suppose we'll be on our way then."

Cindy's heart fell. She pressed her lips together and bit down on her tongue. There were so many retorts balancing on its tip, but it wasn't how she really felt. The downcast expression on his face was enough to push all the whip-smart replies from her mind and in their place was nothing but sadness. He was right. They'd been each other's world for so long, but she'd moved on. He'd never given himself that chance — he'd been fighting so hard to not be seen as the bad guy, he'd forgotten to look for healing.

"Stop," she said, reaching for his arm and halting his escape. "I'm sorry. I didn't think you'd care."

He sighed. "I don't know why. I've told you many times how I feel about you, Cindy. You're important to me, you always will be. It's hurtful the way you're so ready to get rid of me."

"You were the one who walked away," she reminded him.

"I know, and I'll always regret that. But it's time for us to find a new way of living, that doesn't involve us never crossing paths. We live in the same town, we're part of the same family, we have to get along. And I'd prefer we did that as friends, rather than enemies. You and Athol both told me you'd forgiven me after the wedding, and again on Christmas Eve, so I believed we'd put all the rubbish behind us."

"I want us to be friends," she admitted, "but I guess we aren't done healing yet."

He rested a hand on her shoulder. "I'm happy for you — both of you. You and Athol are good together, I can see that now. I'm glad you've found each other. You both deserve love and happiness. You're the two best people in the world, as far as I'm concerned."

She glanced at Athol, who watched them both with quiet interest over the rims of his half-moon spectacles, the news-paper still open between his hands. He smiled at her and dipped his head.

"Thank you, Andy. That means a lot to both me and Athol." She embraced her ex-husband, her head resting against his shoulder. It was a familiar place, a space that'd been a refuge for her once, then a torment as the years progressed and his lies deepened. Regardless of all of that, she could forgive and forget; it was the only way she'd be able to live with peace in her heart, given that he'd be forever a part of her life.

"I can't promise we'll never have ugly feelings come up again, but I will promise to try." She offered him a wry smile.

"That's good enough for me," Andy replied. He looked at Athol. "What do you say, mate?"

Athol cocked his head to one side. "I think it's time I restocked the Scotch."

Andy laughed. "I'll drink to that the next time we come to stay."

"What?" exclaimed Cindy, her heart in her mouth.

Andy grinned. "Just kidding."

She let out a sigh of relief. "Don't do that to me, I might have a heart condition. You don't want to responsible for my death, do you?"

His eyes narrowed. "This is the first I'm hearing of it."

"You didn't know?"

"I heard you had high blood pressure. I think Sarah told me. But who doesn't?"

She sighed. "I'm fine, I'll let you know if we find out anything more."

He offered her his trademark grin, the one that'd swept her off her feet so many decades ago but now only reminded her of broken promises and grief-filled days.

After Andy and Keisha had left, and the kitchen was finally clean, Cindy wandered through the house, picking up bits and pieces that'd been pushed, fallen, or dropped here and there over the holiday period. It didn't take much to straighten up, and when she was done, she looked for Athol whom she found seated at the outside table looking over the backyard, waiting for her with a pot of tea.

"There you are," he said. "I was about to come looking for you."

"A cup of tea, just what I need," she said, claiming the seat next to him.

He smiled and poured her tea, then added milk, just the way she liked it.

"I thought we could work on a small puzzle together," he said.

"Great idea."

He pulled a box off the empty seat beside him and set it on the table. The cover held a photograph of a bridge over a narrow river that glowed gold and pink beneath a sunset. He emptied the pieces onto the table, and Cindy began her search for the corner pieces. She always liked to start with the corners, the edges, then worked her way in.

"Marcus and Anna will be here tomorrow," she said. "For our late Christmas celebration with them."

He grunted in response.

"I've been thinking," she continued. "If you want to give them money to help buy a house, I support you. We'll manage it all somehow."

He lay one hand over hers on the table. "Thank you. You're a good, kind person, and I love you."

"I love you too."

"But I told Marcus I'd help him get the financing with the bank, rather than give him the money. And he was fine with it."

Her eyes widened. "Really? Because I want you to do what you think's best."

"This is what I think is best. He's made some bad choices in his life and it's important he learns from them. I'll sign for the loan, get him a good rate of interest, and if they get into trouble down the road, we can revisit this conversation."

"That sounds like a wise plan," she said, relief tinging her words.

"Thank you, and I appreciate you supporting me," he said, leaning over to kiss her cheek. He cupped her face between his hands, staring into her eyes. His glistened with unshed tears. "It's so nice to have someone to share my life with again after all these years."

She swallowed around a lump in her throat. "I feel the same way."

When he kissed her, all her fears and anxieties drifted away. Whatever came, they'd face it together. He was the partner she'd always longed for. He cared about her and came to her for advice, even when she didn't say what he wanted her to. He was measured and wise, careful before leaping, all the things she'd wished Andy had been. And as they worked on the puzzle together, contentment drifted into her soul.

CHAPTER 20

27TH DECEMBER

ADELE

*C*hristmas was over, and Adele was tired. She pumped the pedals on her bike and stifled a yawn at the same time. Between the family get togethers, helping Sarah with baby Leo and everything going on at the cafe, she hadn't gotten much sleep over the past few weeks. She stood up on the pedals to crest the small rise onto her childhood street, then flew down the length of the street to where Sarah and Mick's house stood.

It was a regal old house, set back on a sweeping circular drive. The gardens had been immaculate, but now had an unkempt look about them. Mick's truck was parked in front of the garden shed, and Sarah's car in the driveway.

She leaned her bike against the bottom of the stairs, and climbed to the front door to knock. No one answered, so she turned the knob and stuck her head through the doorway. She didn't want to yell in case Leo was sleeping. She heard movement at the back of the house, so tip-toed inside and shut the door behind her.

Making as little noise as possible, she crept along the hallway and stopped when she reached the kitchen. Mick was there, making a pot of coffee, his hair ruffled, dressed in work clothes and socks.

"Good morning," she said.

His eyebrows arched. "Oh, hi Adele. I didn't know you were here."

"Just got here," she said, sliding onto a barstool.

"Coffee?"

"Yes, please."

He poured her a cup and pushed it across the bench. "So, what do you have planned today?"

"I'm working at the cafe. I wanted to borrow something from Sarah first."

"Okay, well have fun," he replied, pouring coffee into a travel mug. "Sarah's upstairs having a shower. I'm out of here. I'll see you later."

He left and she sipped her coffee, enjoying the soft morning light that dappled the back deck through the large, glass doors. The hum of air-conditioning filled the silence. Oscar tapped through the house, his toenails loud against the timber floors. He found her, tail wagging and licked her leg.

"You're getting old, buddy. You didn't even hear me come in." He nestled into her leg, tail thumping against her.

Upstairs, she found Sarah half dressed, standing in her closet.

"Good morning, sis," she said, throwing herself onto Sarah's unmade bed with a sigh.

"Hi," replied Sarah. "Did I know you were coming over?" She found a shirt and pulled it over her head.

"Nope. I wanted to see if I could borrow your Pictionary."

Sarah laughed. "Uh, okay. What do you need that for?"

With a sigh, Adele explained the issues she'd been having at the cafe and the way the staff members spent so much of their time bickering or complaining about one another. She'd had a stern word with them once and it'd helped, but it hadn't fixed the issue entirely.

"I thought we could do some team building, see if we can get some of the tension sorted out."

Sarah stood in front of the bathroom mirror to brush her straight brown hair. It snapped and crackled with each vigorous brush stroke. Adele had often been jealous of the way her sister's hair shone. She was effortlessly elegant, something Adele had never managed.

"I don't think Pictionary is the answer, honey."

Adele grunted. "You're probably right."

Sarah set down the brush and walked to the bed, sitting next to Adele. "Have you tried getting them to talk to each other?"

"Not really."

"I think you should try that first, before you resort to board games." Sarah ruffled Adele's hair. Then grimaced. "Why are you bathed in sweat?"

"I rode my bike here."

"Ah, okay." She wiped her hand on a towel in the bathroom, then got to work applying moisturiser to her face and neck.

Adele wandered in to stand beside her. "Why is it you always look so amazing? It's really not fair."

Sarah laughed. "You're crazy. But thank you, that's very sweet."

"I'm serious. My hair is always a little bit frizzy, and I can't ever seem to put an outfit together."

Sarah leaned against the bathroom sink and looked her over. "You could do with a bit of a makeover."

"Yes!" exclaimed Adele, suddenly certain of what she needed. Sarah was effortlessly chic, perhaps Adele could have a little bit of that magic rub off on her. She clapped her hands together. "I need a makeover. Will you give me one, please?"

* * *

HALF AN HOUR LATER, Adele wore a simple, spaghetti strap jumpsuit in sky blue. Her blonde hair was loosely curled and Sarah had given her a natural but stylish look with a some foundation, blush and shiny lip gloss.

"Perfect," said Sarah, taking a step back to survey her handiwork. "You look fantastic."

Adele admired her reflection in the mirror. "Wow, that's impressive. I should come over here everyday for you to dress me."

Sarah rolled her eyes. "Don't you dare."

"How's the planning for the book tour?" asked Adele, slipping her feet into a pair of flats Sarah had lent her.

The baby monitor on the bedside table squawked. Then was filled with the delightful sound of baby noises followed by crying.

"There's Leo," said Sarah, sitting on the bed again to pull on her shoes. "He's finally starting to get into a kind of sleep routine."

"You're looking a little better rested," admitted Adele.

"Thanks to you," said Sarah, with a grin. "You really helped me get back on track."

"That's what I'm here for."

"And the book tour has been changed to a virtual one. I'll be on live video, and I can do readings and giveaways and so on, all from the comfort of my office. I know it's not exactly the same thing as being there, and I can't sign books or really interact with the fans. But for now, it's all I'm willing to commit to. Leo's my priority, and I'm not comfortable leaving Mick here and taking Leo all over the countryside."

They walked together to Leo's room. Sarah scooped him up and kissed his forehead. Adele's heart surged with love for her nephew. He couldn't be any more adorable if he tried. "I think that's a good idea."

"The publisher's tour planner called yesterday to tell me they'd agreed to my plan. I was so relieved. I've been dreading the tour but now I'm actually excited about it."

* * *

WHEN ADELE WALKED into the cafe a few minutes later, Brooke was waiting tables, her blonde hair swinging in a long ponytail down her back.

She grinned at Adele as she balanced a stack of plates in one hand. "Looking fine Adele!"

Adele's entire face flushed with warmth. She waved a hand. "Thanks Brooke. Sarah did a makeover."

"Well, it's working for you."

In the kitchen, Francesca did a double take. She stopped slicing avocados and pressed both hands to her ample hips. "I love that colour on you. Blue is definitely your hue."

"Well, thank you Franny."

"You're welcome, honey. The linen order came in."

"Finally!" exclaimed Adele with relief. If it hadn't come in today she had planned on visiting the Food Store to buy up their stock of napkins and paper towels.

She spun to press a hand to the top of the linen order, which sat in several boxes against one wall. Smiled. Then, skipped off to her office to prepare for the day ahead.

Adele buried herself in paperwork, attempting to catch

up after the busyness of the Christmas holidays. They wouldn't get a break, since they'd move right into the New Year, and the peak summer season — which was the busiest time of the year in the Cove. But this morning things seemed to be relatively quiet and under control, and she planned to take advantage of the break to get the stacks of papers on her desk and the unread emails in her inbox, under control.

It wasn't long before she was interrupted by a knock at the door. Francesca poked her head through the gap.

"Is it a bad time?"

"No, come on in," replied Adele, grateful for the chance to take a break from paying bills.

Francesca sat in a chair opposite the desk and crossed her feet at the ankles.

"How can I help you?" opened Adele, sensing the older woman's reluctance to speak.

Francesca cleared her throat. "Uh… well, I wanted to talk to you about Brooke and Crystal."

"Okay." She knew where this was going and her heart sank. She'd hoped the tension between the staff had lifted. Although she had to admit that kind of thinking was more wishful than anything else.

"They're out of control. They do whatever they like. They have no respect for the kitchen, or for me. They play their music at full volume, and roll their eyes when I ask them to turn it down." Francesca's cheeks were red.

"I'm sorry to hear that," replied Adele. "Why don't I call them in now and we can have a talk?"

Francesca shifted in place. "Uh, well I don't know if that's necessary."

"Yes, I think it is." She hurried from the office, through the kitchen and into the cafe. There was only one customer, Samuel. He sat at a small table with a chess board between himself and Eddy, who perched on the opposite seat. He was sipping an iced tea, but otherwise had ordered nothing more. He could do without the wait staff for a few minutes.

"Brooke and Crystal, could you come with me please?" She called.

Both waitresses followed her back to the office. The looked uncomfortable when they saw Francesca seated there.

"Come in, come in. I'm sorry there aren't enough seats for you all, but this won't take long. I want us all to have a quick talk about the issues we're all experiencing. I know you love the cafe and want it to be a positive and affirming workplace, as much as I do. Let's find a way forward so we can have that."

Crystal leaned against the wall and crossed her arms over her chest. Brooke smacked a piece of gum between her teeth, then sighed.

"Great, I'm glad we're all on the same page," continued Adele, taking her seat behind the desk. "Franny tells me that there are a few things you two are doing that bother her. Do you know what those things are?"

Both waitresses nodded mutely.

"Great, so do you think you could stop doing those things?"

Another round of nods.

"Is there anything you'd like to ask of Francesca?"

Brooke's eyes flashed. "She bosses us around. It seems like she hates us, the way she speaks to us. It's like we don't matter to her at all."

"I do not!" exclaimed Francesca, coming to her feet.

Adele waved her back into her seat. "I hear what you're saying. Do you feel the same way, Crystal?"

Crystal shrugged. "I guess."

"If the two of you can agree not to irritate Franny so much, then perhaps she can agree to talk to you in a kinder way. What do you think Franny?"

Francesca huffed. "I don't hate them."

"I know you don't. But if they're struggling with your tone, maybe you could try using a different approach."

"Fine, I suppose I can do that."

"Great, I'm glad to hear it. I need all of you to treat each other with respect and consideration. We're a team and we should act like it. Franny is in charge of everything whenever I'm not here. And even when I am, she's my second in charge, so everyone else has to do what she says. However, she's going to try to take a gentler approach to the way she manages you. That being said, I won't stand for back-stabbing, criticisms, snark or conflict in our workplace. And since we're talking about work related issues, I need you all to try to make it to every shift and to give me as much notice as possible if you can't. When you back out at the last minute, it leaves me scrambling and the cafe suffers. So, unless you're unwell, please try to make it to work when you've committed to do so. Does everyone understand?"

All three of the women indicated their agreement. She dismissed the meeting and they shuffled from the office. Adele drew a deep breath the moment they were gone. She wasn't sure if she'd taken the right approach, but the words had tumbled from her mouth and she felt good about it.

"We'll see how that goes," she muttered beneath her breath, as she got back to work.

By the time she'd finished for the day, she would've been happy never to look at another computer screen again for the rest of her life. She shut the computer down, locked the office and headed out through the almost empty cafe.

"Can you shut up for me tonight please, Franny?" She called as she went. Franny called out her agreement, and Adele stepped into the humid afternoon. A faint breeze rippled off the ocean, lifting her hair from her shoulders.

"Hi there," said Carlos. He'd walked up from the beach in

a pair of board shorts, and was dripping wet. His black hair was plastered to his head. His brown eyes twinkled.

"Hi," she said. She was surprised and excited to see him. "Having a swim?"

He grinned, leaning down to kiss her softly. The movement stole her breath away and left her with drips of salty water on her lips.

"Yep. I thought I'd come and see if you're willing to make good on your promise."

"My promise?" She cupped a hand over her eyes to shield them from the glare of the sun. "What promise was that?"

"To take me surfing."

"That's right — I said I would, didn't I?"

"You did." He stood close, her heart shimmied against her ribcage.

She grinned. "I've got a couple of surfboards in the back of the store room. I keep them there for the times I want to surf after work."

"Perfect, I'll help you get them," he said.

"Uh, you'll drip on my floor. Wait here, I'll bring them out."

She hurried to the back room and quickly changed into a bikini and wetsuit, then grabbed one of the surfboards to carry outside. She fetched the second board next, and soon they were on the beach, studying the break. She showed him where the rip could be found, where the best surf was, and how to hold and stand on the board.

When they paddled out to the break, she admired the strength of his arms, the ripple of muscles across his tanned back. A smile flitted across her face. There was something comforting about him. Spending time together felt like coming home.

He'd introduced her to his family, wasn't ashamed of her. He'd met her family too, and seemed to sincerely enjoy their company. He'd helped with her Christmas tree, and gone shopping with her. Antoine had never gone out in public with her, had hidden her away from everyone as though he was ashamed. Which of course, he was. She knew that now. But being with Carlos was freeing. They could laugh together, walk hand in hand, go to restaurants, and not have to worry about who might see them.

It wasn't like any relationship she'd experienced before. She could be herself — completely sincere. She didn't feel as though she had to pretend, or wear a mask. It was invigorating. He'd brought her heart back to life. And she couldn't wait to spend more time with him.

"Here you go, this is your wave!" She shouted, as a swell rose behind them.

He paddled ahead of the wave and took off. When he tried to stand, he fell headfirst into the water. She paddled after him, laughing.

"Good try," she said, as he broke the surface coughing.

She patted him on the back and he laughed, reaching for the board. "That was fun, let's go again."

CHAPTER 21

ADELE

The riverboat bobbed gently on the rippling surface of the dark water. Adele's flats slapped on the timber boards as they walked side by side towards the boat. Her hand ached to slip into Carlos's, but their relationship was so new she was anxious. It was silly to be so scared, but she couldn't help it. There was something special about this man — she didn't want to ruin it, not when she wasn't sure exactly how he felt about her. He was so quiet most of the time, and his face didn't reveal a lot about what was going on inside his head. But he'd asked her to spend New Year's Eve with him after their surf, so she took that as a good sign.

"We're going on a boat?" she asked.

"Not just a boat, a river cruise." He held out a hand to help her aboard. She climbed down the few steps onto the boat and wandered along the deck behind a line of other people to

187

an open-air seating area lit by twinkle lights and lanterns, and with soft instrumental music playing in the background.

He'd kept their date a surprise from her, but suggested she wear something comfortable. She'd bought a new pair of slacks and an open neck white silk blouse for the occasion. She'd even curled her hair and put on makeup.

"You look amazing!" Sarah had gushed when she'd swung by to leave a casserole for their dinner. "The student has become the master. It's so good to see you getting out and having some fun. I'm glad you're moving on with your life. You deserve to be happy." Sarah's voice choked as she hugged Adele.

Adele had walked away, her throat aching. She was moved by her sister's words and her compassion. Until that moment, she hadn't realised how much she'd slipped into a funk after what happened in Darwin. Sure, she'd spent plenty of days lying in bed when she could've been out and about. She'd hardly surfed in months. And she'd lost weight. But still, she'd never really believed things were that bad. She was sad, that was all. Wasn't it natural to be sad after a relationship breakdown?

But seeing Sarah's face light up when she opened the door, dispelled all of Adele's self-talk in a single moment. She'd been drowning and her family knew it. Now, she'd found her way to shore, was gulping great mouthfuls of fresh oxygen, and it showed. She was on her way to being happy — being herself — again.

The setting sun burnished the water like fire. A cool breeze filtered over the river, drifting into the boat, and chasing away the cloying humidity. Adele and Carlos stood by the railing at the very back of the boat, looking downstream.

"It's beautiful," she said.

"I'm glad you like it."

"It's very romantic," she admitted even as her cheeks grew hot. Vulnerability was hard for her, but she wanted to be open, to give him a chance to touch her heart even if in the end it only hurt. She didn't want to give up on love. Not yet.

He slipped his hand over hers, feeling her fingers one by one with his own, and a bolt of energy flickered up her arm and through her body. It was like a dream, this moment. So much energy, hope, attraction, and passion all curled up inside her, ready to spring forth. He did this to her, made her forget her reluctance, her pain. Made her want to leap into his arms. It was disconcerting and dizzying all at the same time.

The boat pulled away from the jetty with all the passengers milling about on two levels — an upper and lower deck. Waiters dressed in white shirts and black pants carried trays of drinks. Adele reached for one and gulped down a mouthful of bubbling champagne. It tickled her nostrils, almost made her sneeze. She held it in, instead drawing a deep breath of the fresh, cool air.

"This river reminds me of something," said Carlos.

She faced him, the fingers of one hand still entwined in his. "Oh?"

"I don't know exactly what it is. A memory from my childhood. Something to do with my grandparents and riding on a boat along a river like this one. It brings up sadness in me, but I'm not sure why." He smiled. "Do you ever have half-formed memories like that?"

"All the time," she said. "Things trigger a memory, but you can't quite reel it in. Like it's bobbing out there on the water's surface and you recognise it, but you can't get it to come any closer."

"That's exactly it," he admitted. "Thanks for putting it into words for me."

"Why do you think you were sad?"

He shrugged. "It's how I was. For most of my life, I've lived with this sadness and guilt hanging over me."

She frowned. "That's terrible."

"My mother died when she was chasing me around a park. I remember running away from her because I didn't want to go home yet and her calling my name. She was frustrated because I wasn't listening, and then she was in pain and collapsed. So, I suppose I've always felt guilt about that. And my grandparents were so sad when that happened, especially after leaving their homeland and everyone else they loved behind. I picked up on that. We weren't a very lively bunch when I was a kid. I tried to get away on my own as much as I could, probably because of that."

"I'm sorry," she said, with a shake of her head. "I wish I could've been there to give you a hug."

"So do I," he replied.

"But you're not sad now?"

"No, not anymore. It's as though a veil has lifted off my life. I know it sounds crazy, but when I met you, I was sleep walking through my days. You've brought me to life in a way I didn't believe was possible. I thought it was my personality, that I was destined to be different to everyone else, to never have that passion for life. I wanted it, but it was never there. Until I met you."

She grinned, her throat aching over what he'd told her. "I feel the same way about you. I'd had my heart broken and I wasn't sure I could recover from that. But you've helped me see that there's a way forward, a way out of that pain."

Her gaze dropped to the boat, her face flushing with warmth. She wasn't used to being so open, so vulnerable with anyone. Usually, she kept her feelings and thoughts to herself. It was why she'd waited so long to tell her family about the problems she had in Darwin. Too long. Looking back, she could see that now. She should've faced what was happening much sooner, gotten out of there earlier. She'd allowed herself to sit and stew in the hopelessness of her situation, allowed Antoine to continue to manipulate and take advantage when she should've walked away. She didn't want to keep everything bottled up inside herself anymore. She wanted to be free and open. Carlos brought that out in her. He was stoic, strong, and compassionate. She felt safe with him as though she could tell him anything and be herself completely. He'd never manipulate her or abuse her trust.

He raised her face, until her gaze met his, with one finger beneath her chin. "I didn't feel at home in my own life. But now I know I can have a life, a full life, even after everything my family has been through. And I want that. With you."

His words set her heart pounding. Her head felt light. She'd never felt this way about anyone before, not even Antoine. The things he was saying, they weren't the kind of thing she'd ever heard spoken to her. She wasn't used to this kind of adoration, and it woke something up inside of her, with a fluttering in her belly she couldn't control. Then he kissed her and her mind emptied of every thought.

They ate dinner at small tables dotted along the boat deck. Adele and Carlos sat on the top deck, with the wind blowing Adele's hair across her face as she ate. She laughed and attempted to tuck it into her collar. The river was pock-marked by ripples as the wind hurried across its surface. All around them, couples were engaged in conversation, held hands, or stood in a loose embrace at the railing to look out over the water. Gentle laughter rippled across the deck. Close to the cabin, a duo performed cover songs. A woman played keyboard while a man sang and strummed a guitar.

The upbeat tunes had Adele's foot tapping beneath the table as she ate a last mouthful of creme brûlée.

She leaned back in her chair with a sigh. "That was delicious. And I'm completely and utterly full."

Carlos smiled. "Are you sure, because this chocolate mud cake is amazing, and I can't eat it all."

Her eyes widened. "Well, maybe I could have one bite.

He reached forward with his fork and gently pushed a large bite of cake into her mouth. She chewed slowly, savouring the heavy, decadent desert. "Wow, you're right," she muttered around a mouthful. "I should've ordered the cake."

"You can finish mine. It's too rich for my taste."

She happily accepted the plate. "Nothing is too rich for my taste. At least, if there is something that qualifies, I haven't found it yet."

Carlos laughed. "I'll keep that in mind."

She was eating like a pig, but she couldn't bring herself to care in that moment. For months she'd hardly eaten. Mum complained she was fading away. But now, her appetite was back, and she was happy to indulge it.

"I start my new job the day after tomorrow," he said.

She swallowed a mouthful of cake. "I'm sure you'll be great."

"Thanks. Maybe we could meet up afterwards, I could come to the cafe?"

"I'd like that." She couldn't express in words how good it felt to be dating a man who was willing to tell her how he felt about her, to take her out in public, to get to know her family. She hadn't noticed the way Antoine hid her away from prying eyes at first but looking back she could see how wrong it'd all been. Everything in secret, no public dates in places anyone might recognise them. He cancelled on her so often at the last moment, she came to expect it. But not with

Carlos. He reached for her hand and held it across the table. He was ready to show her he cared, to meet her at work, to take her out on romantic dates.

After dinner, they stood at the railing to watch a fireworks show. As the fireworks exploded in a dazzling display over the river, with the cityscape as a backdrop through the dark night, Carlos stood behind Adele and linked his arms around her. He kissed the top of her head and she leaned back into him, resting her head on his chest.

She was content.

She'd come so far since she left Darwin. A new career, a new place to live. And now someone special to share her life with. She spun slowly in his arms and watched as the fireworks flashed and shone, reflected in Carlos's dark eyes.

"I'm not big on new year's resolutions," she said. "Instead, I like to think about what I'm grateful for. What's gone right over the year."

He tightened his grip around her waist. "Oh? What are you grateful for?"

"I'm thankful for being home, for my family who've been there for me through all the hard stuff. I'm grateful for a job I love, and a second chance at happiness. I'm thankful for the beach, the waves, and the air in my lungs. And I'm thankful for you."

He grinned. "I'm grateful for you as well."

As the clock ticked over to the new year, the people around them shouted, "Happy New Year" while the fireworks continued.

"Happy New Year," said Carlos, his gaze drifting to her lips.

Her heart thudded and she stood on tiptoe, reaching for him. "Happy New Year, and many more to come."

Their kiss ignited fireworks within her to match those behind them. She combed her fingers through his hair, cupping the back of his neck and pulling him to her. Her mind raced over the year that'd passed, everything she'd been through, the difficulty, the pain, the humiliation. Then, she remembered the warmth of a family that welcomed her home and helped her back on her feet. The love of a community who never gave up on her, who didn't judge her mistakes and who offered her another chance to build the kind of life she'd always wanted. And she smiled against Carlos' lips, as she imagined all the good things a future together might bring.

THE END

EXCERPT FROM THE WARATAH INN

BOOK 1, THE WARATAH INN SERIES

By Lilly Mirren

* * *

Read the series in order:

The Waratah Inn
One Summer in Italy
The Summer Sisters

Christmas at the Waratah Inn
(a standalone novel)

ABOUT THE BOOK

Wrested back to Cabarita Beach by her grandmother's sudden death, Kate Summer discovers a mystery buried in the past that changes everything.

When Kate returns home to the sleepy hamlet of Cabarita Beach and the run-down Waratah Inn where she spent many happy childhood years, all she wants to do is sell the dilapidated boutique inn and head back to the city and her busy, professional life. But she and her two estranged sisters discover they've inherited the inn together. To sell, they need all three sisters to agree to the sale.

When things in her carefully constructed life begin to unravel, Kate decides to stay in Cabarita Beach to renovate the elegant, old building. Despite her misgivings about reviving the crumbling structure, she soon becomes consumed with crown moulding, history and an attractive horse wrangler she just can't seem to ignore.

When she discovers a clue to a mystery from the past in her grandmother's things, she'll be drawn down a path that raises more questions than answers. Piece-by-piece she and her sisters will uncover the secret former life of their beloved grandmother. A life of love, intrigue, and loss. A life they never knew she had.

When the three sisters have the opportunity to sell the Inn, they'll have a decision to make: commit to the Waratah Inn and family, or walk away from the Inn and each other, back to their separate and isolated lives.

The first book in a continuing series of four.

CHAPTER 1

AUGUST 1995

BRISBANE

*T*he wind clutched at Kate Summer's straight, brown hair blowing it in wild bursts around her head and into her green eyes. The ferry lurched forward. She grabbed onto a cold, metal handrail with one hand and held her flyaway hair against her neck with the other. Then she stepped through the doorway and into the City Ferry cabin. The rush of wind in her ears quieted, replaced by the dull murmur of conversation between commuters as they huddled together in clumps throughout the cabin.

The Kangaroo Point terminal faded out of sight behind them as the ferry chugged across the sluggish, brown Brisbane River towards the city centre. Kate tugged her coat tighter around her body and inhaled a steadying breath through her reddened nose. It'd once been smattered with freckles, but time had faded them to a pale remnant of their former selves.

Sighing, she sank into one of the hard chairs that were

lined up like so many church pews, smoothed her hair with one hand as best she could, and set her purse on the empty seat beside her.

She had to get to work on time today. Marco was stressed out about the new menu. He'd called her at home to tell her he wasn't entirely convinced it was a good idea to take the restaurant in a new direction, what with the economic climate the way it was. She reminded him the economic climate was fine and it was the perfect time to try something new, as they'd discussed a hundred times over the past six months. That he'd named her head chef at the *Orchid* for a reason and should listen to her ideas.

He'd agreed and hung up. But she'd heard the tension in his voice. He hated change. She knew that well enough, having worked for him for five years. But five years of creating food that was expected, safe, the same as it had always been, was more than enough for her. If he didn't want to make the change, then she would. Her creative spirit itched for something different.

The ferry pulled to a stop, growling back and forth until its ramp lined up with the dock. When she stepped onto solid ground, she couldn't help one wistful glance back at the river. She missed the water. The ocean had been like a second home to her once. She'd spent so much of her teenage years diving under the waves, floating on her back, and staring up at the sky on a calm day, or surfing the break when the wind was up. But since she didn't live near the beach these days, she had to make do with the river. It wasn't the same but paddling a kayak or riding the ferry brought a measure of peace.

By the time she reached the restaurant, she'd already run over the menu again in her mind and was convinced they were doing the right thing by reinvigorating their offerings.

It was fresh, unique, delicious — it would bring diners into the restaurant in droves. She was sure of it.

Or it would drive them away.

Her stomach tightened at the thought of what Marco would say if it didn't work the way she hoped it would. Reputation was everything for a chef, and in a small city like Brisbane, failures weren't something you could hide.

"Morning chef." Her Sous Chef greeted her with a warm smile. "Ready to change the world?"

She chuckled. "Ready as I'll ever be."

Fresh groceries from the market lined one of the bench tops along the wall. She always placed her orders the day before. Fresh produce, direct from the farmers, was the best way to make delicious meals, and the write-ups she'd received so far in the local newspapers showed it. She'd sent one review to Nan.

What she really wanted to do was drive down to Cabarita and bring Nan back with her, so her grandmother could taste the food for herself. Not that she was such a big fan of Asian fusion cuisine. Nan preferred her meat and three veg, like most Australians of her generation. Still, Kate wanted her to see the restaurant, see the career she'd built for herself over the past decade. She was proud of what she'd achieved and wanted someone to share that with.

Just thinking of Nan and the inn put a twist in her gut. She hadn't been back to see Nan in months, and when she'd gone the last time she'd only visited briefly. Nan had made her promise to stay longer on the next trip, but with everything she had going on, the visit never happened.

If the new menu didn't work out, Kate would have plenty of time on her hands to visit Nan and the Waratah Inn. Maybe she'd be a permanent guest there. She shook her head, her pulse accelerating as worry over the future, her career, and personal life washed over her again. She was used to it, this anxiety. It clogged her thoughts, put knots in her gut and sent waves of adrenaline coursing through her veins.

The new menu *had* to work. It was the first time Marco had given her complete control over what they'd serve. If people didn't like it, he might never offer her the chance again.

She wasn't ready to concede defeat and move in with her grandmother yet. But a holiday, a beach holiday, was a great idea. Davis had been bugging her about getting away together, away from the city and their crazy, hectic schedules, ever since he proposed six months earlier. She'd suggest it when she saw him that night after work. They often met up late for a light meal, since she worked when most people were done for the day. He didn't like it, but what could she do? It was her career. He'd said they should take a vacation, but they hadn't spoken of it since. Perhaps it was time to raise the subject together. They could both do with some time off. And more than that, she missed Nan.

CHAPTER 2

AUGUST 1995

CABARITA BEACH

*T*he sand squelched between her toes, wetting the soles of her feet with a cold that sent a shiver up her spine. The grittiness of it, the scent of salt in the air, the warmth of the sun on her face — all were familiar feelings, sensations she'd grown to love. It'd taken time to embrace this place, but she had. For years now, it'd been home.

Home.

The word reverberated through her soul and her smile lingered as she brushed the strands of white hair from her eyes. When had it turned white? She'd have described it as blonde with silver highlights not so long ago. Now there wasn't any blonde left; it was more the colour of snow.

It'd taken an age to allow herself to call it home here. Home had been so far away. Such a different place, a different time. But this was Edie Summer's home now. Adjusting to change was part of life, though some changes you never grew accustomed to.

Even her name had once been foreign to her, had caused a little pain in her heart that couldn't be shaken whenever anyone called her by it. "Have a nice day, Mrs. Summer," they'd say, and her stomach would clench. "Nice weather we're having, Mrs. Summer," and her head would spin as pin pricks of light danced before her eyes. Now, her name was as familiar to her as the lines that lingered on her face long after her smile had faded.

A pair of seagulls trotted along in front of her, just out of reach. Their red-rimmed eyes watched close as each head craned from side to side, feet scampering in a steady rhythm. She picked up the pace and they launched into the air, a rapid flapping of wings taking them above her head in no time, their cries drifting back to her on the breeze.

She watched them go, her eyes squinting against the glare of the rising sun. One hand tented against her forehead, her gaze followed them out over the spray of a dark wave, then they disappeared into the bright colours of the sunrise.

Pink, orange, and yellow. Glowing fingers reached from the horizon towards her, shooting bright blue lights high into the sky overhead. It was beautiful in a way that made her heart sigh. How many more of these would she see? How many had she ignored or simply slept through in her youth?

She glanced along the length of the beach, studying the dark outline of Castle Rock as the dawn pulled it from the shadows, surrounded by froth and bubbles. A wave hurtled itself at the rock, and salt spray shot into the air, raining down in droplets on its black surface.

Perching on that rock was one of the things she'd loved to do most, back when scrambling out beyond the waves wasn't such a chore. She'd dive beneath the curling lip, water rushing against her ears and pummelling her body. Then both feet would plant in the sand and her head would break free of the water's surface as she gasped for breath, in time for the next breaker to lean over her.

A frown creased her forehead. That was before her body slowed and diving through waves became a hazard, or at least that's what Jemima told her. Back when so many things were easier to do. Maybe she should never have given it up. Mima had become too cautious, except when it came to love. She wasn't cautious about love.

Edie smiled and let her eyes drift shut a moment, the sun playing a kaleidoscope of lights through her eyelids. A play formed in her mind as the lights danced, the cast so familiar to her and yet seeming unreal in their youthful beauty, with broad smiles on handsome faces. Smiles unchecked yet by grief, suffering or loss. Smiles full of love and the prospect of life to come.

Her own smile drooped as one image filled her mind's eye. His face was no longer so clear as it once had been. Wisps and vapours gave him smudged edges and his eyes, at one time so clear to her, seemed distant. Still, her heart squeezed as memories poured over her like deep water through narrowed shores.

With a cough she cleared her throat and her eyes blinked open, taking a moment to adjust to the burgeoning daylight. So many memories. She could spend the entire day wrapped up in them and never leave the beach, but there were things to do. Always something needing her attention.

She pushed a hand into one of the pockets of her loose-fitting culottes, searching, and pulled free a piece of paper, a newspaper clipping. An article about a chef in Brisbane whose restaurant had surprised the critic with its vibrancy and unique artistry. "A breath of fresh air," he'd written — a cliché but it'd warmed her heart, nonetheless. She read it again in a whisper, repeating the words over as one finger traced the outline of her granddaughter's cheek.

Kate was so beautiful, as all her granddaughters were. So much like her father, in so many ways. Edie's eyes misted, and she swatted at them with the back of her hand and with the impatience of having cried too many tears too many times.

Her stomach clenched and she wondered if the milk she'd added to her coffee that morning had been too far gone after all. Bile rose up her throat. She shook off a dizzy feeling and strode through the sand, shoving the article back into her pocket as she went.

There were guests to wait on, people to serve, rooms to tend. Not so many as there'd been in years gone by, but still, they were there, and they needed her. The life of an innkeeper was never dull.

It wasn't a life she would've chosen in her youth. She'd had so many dreams for herself back then, but that was before her eyes had been opened by horror and violence, to the possibility that life should be more than what others laid out for you like freshly ironed clothes on the bed.

When she was young, all she'd known was the path followed by her mother, grandmother and the generations of women that surrounded her then. She knew what she would be, and she relished the thought. Treasured it. Looked forward to a life of domesticity in the town of her birth, with icy winds nipping at her nose and children mewling at her breast.

Then she'd grown, and her dreams had grown with her. A career, something for herself. A path to sharpen the mind and leave behind a legacy. It was difficult to remember exactly what it was that had driven her. Likely the same energy and optimism imbued in young people everywhere before the world snatched it away.

Puffing lightly, she stepped out of the sand and onto a hard-packed trail through the dunes. It wound, rose, and fell, soon becoming a track of loosely connected timber slats, dusted with sand that rose and rose towards the green hillock ahead.

When she reached the hillock, she paused to catch her breath. Walking had become more difficult in recent days. She'd done so much of it in her life she had no desire to slow down now. She knew how to push through the pain. To keep going even when she didn't feel like it.

With one calloused palm resting on a handrail made of sun-bleached timber, she glanced back over her shoulder. The sun had popped over the horizon in its full glory now, remnants of pink glistened within its bright, yellow rays. The entire beach was bathed in light, sand warming, and crabs finding their way back to holes that hid them from the heat of the day. The waves, no longer dark, sparkled azure.

Her breathing slowed and she climbed the stairs at a brisk pace. Sandals awaited her at the top, lined up neatly side by side. She slid her feet into them, then marched through the short grass.

The inn rose tall ahead of her. Shadows from a grove of pandanus mottled the peeling pink paint. The gutter on the rear side of the building sagged and smoke sputtered from the small chimney above it.

She stopped to study the building, inhaled slowly, and smiled to herself. It'd seen better days, but then again, so had she. To her it would always be the place she'd found herself. The place where her wounded heart had discovered a refuge.

Her thoughts returned to her granddaughters. They'd spent years living here, with her. Would they treasure it the way she had, or would they throw it away and go on with their busy lives? She knew she shouldn't care. When she was gone, she'd have no way of knowing what any of them did, or what became of her legacy. Only, she wanted them to find each other again, her wayward girls.

Perhaps she should've told them why it meant so much to her. Already Nyreeda had suggested she sell the place and retire. "Relax," she'd said. "You've worked hard all your life. Sell the inn and get some rest." Bindi was the only one of the three who'd objected. But she'd always been the fondest of the inn, probably because she'd spent the longest part of her childhood within its paint-chipped walls.

Relax. *Pshaw.* What did she know about relaxing?

At some point in your life you had to give up and do what you knew how to do, and she knew how to take care of people. It was what she did, what she loved. They might as well bury her now if she couldn't do that.

But the girls — they didn't understand it. Didn't understand her. And perhaps it wasn't their fault. She'd kept so much of herself from them. Had it been a mistake?

She'd only wanted to protect them. To give them some semblance of stability. But they were grown women now. Maybe it was time. The next visit, she'd sit them down and tell them all about why this inn mattered. How it'd saved her. Why she was the way she was. What she'd been through, what she'd kept hidden. Yes, it was the right time. They were ready, and now she had no reason not to break open the past and let its secrets spill out like stagnant water from an old vase.

* * *

KATE WASHED her hands at the sink, then examined the produce, turning the vegetables over in her hands, her mind running through all they had to get done before service began that evening.

One by one, the kitchen staff filed in. They greeted her, then chatted together as they set about doing their various tasks. She missed the camaraderie of being one of them. She was the boss, and as much as she'd worked to make that happen, she hadn't realised it would be such a lonely job.

The phone on the wall rang, a high-pitched jangle that pierced the air and reverberated off the white, tiled walls. One of the staff answered, then met her gaze with the earpiece extended towards her.

"It's for you, chef."

She set down a bunch of greens with a frown. Who would be calling her at the restaurant? It could be Davis, he didn't call often, but maybe he'd had a change of plans and couldn't meet her tonight for tea. Irritation bristled over her skin. He'd been doing that a lot lately, canceling on her. How did he expect them to enter into a lifetime of wedded bliss if they never saw each other?

She took the phone and pressed it to her ear, already considering the things she'd say to Davis if he canceled again. She'd be calm, mature, but firm. He couldn't keep backing out of their plans last minute, it wasn't fair to her or to them. They were building a life together and he should prioritise that.

She wouldn't raise her voice or let her temper flare up, the last thing she wanted to be was some shrill housewife demanding her future husband spend more time with her. And Dad had always told her she should begin as she intended to go on, in relationships and in business.

She'd be kind, patient, loving, but make sure he understood that she wouldn't stand for second best when it came to their relationship. Either she was his priority, or she wasn't. In her mind it was simple. She hesitated for a moment before speaking. What if he decided she wasn't his priority? Her stomach twisted into a knot.

"Hello? This is Kate Summer."

"Kate? Is that you, Kate?" The soft, wobbling voice threw her.

"Yes, this is Kate. Who is this?"

"Oh good, I'm glad I found you sweetheart. It's Mima, from the inn."

"Mima? Wow, it's good to hear your voice. How are you?" Unexpected tears pricked the back of her throat. She should visit them more often. She hadn't realised how much she missed the entire crew from the inn. After all, it'd been her home once.

"I'm good honey. Not as spry as I once was, and one of my knees has been playing up. But otherwise, I'm fit as a fiddle."

"I'm glad to hear it. I hope everything's okay." Why was Mima Everest calling her at the restaurant in the middle of the day? Her stomach knotted as she waited for Mima's response.

She heard a rustling sound. Mima cleared her throat, soft at first then with a loud, grizzled cough that hacked at her lungs. She was about to speak again, when Mima's voice echoed down the line.

"Look, sweetheart, there's no easy way to say this." Her voice broke, and Kate turned away from the kitchen to face the wall, her breath caught in her throat.

"Your Nan died this morning. She's been having some trouble with her ticker as you know, and she took a walk along the beach, like she always did, but as she was coming up the path to the inn she fell over. Thankfully, Jack saw her and came running to help. We called the ambulance right away, but it was too late I'm afraid. Jack performed CPR, and mouth-to-mouth, he knows about all that stuff from being a lifesaver for years. But she was gone just the same." Mima sniffled and coughed again. "I'm so sorry, sweetheart. I know how much you loved her. We all did."

Kate's breath finally released, and she inhaled again with a sharp intake of breath. "No," she whispered, squeezing her eyes shut.

"Sorry, what was that, love?"

"Nothing, nothing. Thanks for calling to tell me, Mima."

"You okay, sweetheart?"

No, she wasn't. How long had it been since she'd seen Nan's sweet face? Christmas at least. She'd gone to the inn for Christmas but hadn't stayed for New Year. Davis had wanted them to go to some party at one of his colleague's fancy penthouse apartments. Anger burned in her gut. Why hadn't she stayed longer? Nan had asked her to, but she'd turned her down. There was always next year, she'd told herself, only now there wasn't. There never would be again.

"Kate?"

She realised she hadn't answered Mima's question. "I'm... I don't know, Mima. I'm wishing I'd come down there. I didn't know about her heart. Why didn't she tell me?"

Mima sighed. "I thought she had told you. She promised me... but you know your Nan. Stubborn as the day is long." Mima chuckled, but the sound faded away.

The sounds of the kitchen hummed behind her and Kate rested her forehead on the cold wall beside the phone. She squeezed the earpiece until her fingernails dug into the flesh of her palm.

She cleared her throat. "Have you spoken to Reeda or Bindi yet?"

"I talked to Reeda a few minutes ago. I have to dig up Bindi's phone number. I couldn't find her at work. I tried you earlier, but I guess you weren't there. No one answered."

"I just got in," Kate responded.

"That makes sense. Reeda's hopping on a flight to the Gold Coast airport tomorrow morning. I don't know when Bindi will be coming."

Kate's head spun. They were unveiling the new menu; everything was riding on her. Marco was counting on her.

And she had to go to Cabarita Beach to say farewell to her grandmother. Her stomach roiled.

"I guess I'll go home now and pack. It shouldn't take me more than a couple of hours to make the drive. I'll be there before tea."

"Okay, love. I can't wait to see you, sad circumstances notwithstanding."

"You too," Kate replied, numbness filtering through her body.

She hung up the phone, but stayed still, her forehead pressed to the wall. She pushed her hands against it as well, and hovered there for several long moments, willing her body to move.

"You okay, chef?" asked a voice behind her.

She nodded. "Fine." And pushed herself back from the wall.

CHAPTER 3

AUGUST 1995

CABARITA BEACH

*L*eaving the city had frayed Kate's nerves. The ferry ride back to Kangaroo Point. The walk to her unit where the lift wasn't working and she had to climb eight flights of stairs, then leaned, puffing against the door before she could extract her keys from her purse in a haze of oxygen deprivation.

She'd packed a bag without a clear thought. She threw in a bikini before remembering it was the middle of winter and she wasn't likely to want to swim, then thought perhaps she should keep the bikini after all since her surfboard was stored at the inn. She wondered briefly if it was bad form to think about bikinis and surfing when her grandmother had recently died and slumped onto the bed with her hands pressed to her face.

Her thoughts were tangled, and she struggled to extract a strand long and straight enough to focus on getting out the door and into the car. After that, she'd run into a traffic jam, and it'd taken three hours to drive from Brisbane to Cabarita Beach. She'd tried to find a radio station with soothing music to help slow her heart rate, but all she could find was something called *Trance Dance*, and another pumping out a loud, alternative rock song where the vocalist's almost on-pitch nasal growl tugged on her frayed nerves.

She switched off the radio, letting her thoughts wander. Her mind kept flicking through a slideshow of images. Nan in her rocking chair laughing over something she and her sisters had done. Nan marching along the beach in her gumboots, waving a stick at a seagull who'd had the nerve to steal a hot chip from Nan's hand. Nan sitting astride her favourite chestnut mare, then digging in her heels to send the animal into a gallop over the golden sand.

She was only a few minutes away from Cabarita and her pulse accelerated at the thought of what she'd find there. The Waratah Inn, with no Nan.

The sun set in a lazy haze beyond the distant mountains. Shadows lengthened over the straight, narrow road that was called a highway but was really only wide enough for two cars to squeeze by each other with dust and gravel flying up beneath the tires that tickled the edges, and her stomach was clenched in the same knot it had been ever since she took that phone call from Mima.

Rolling dunes undulated towards the blue sky to her left with hardenbergia, dianella, and lomandra plants dotted here and there and lining the uneven edge of the bitumen. To her right, squat casuarina and banksia trees shielded a fragile grassy plain and hid the road from the bulk of the sunset's blinding rays where they shone through the breaks between foliage in bursts.

Kate chewed a fingernail, the other hand holding tight to the steering wheel of her blue Honda CR-V. She'd taken her first trip down this road the year she turned eight. Her parents brought her and her sisters up from Sydney for a visit. They'd hired a car at the airport and taken this road to the inn. She recalled her father's words, as he leaned forward to peer at the narrow stretch of bitumen over the steering wheel, his knuckles white.

"I mean, what were Mum and Dad thinking moving all the way out here? Good Lord! I know I grew up here, but I didn't realise it then: we're in the middle of nowhere. Where are we?" He waved a hand with enthusiastic abandon at the windscreen. "You'd think they'd want to see their grandchildren occasionally, but no. They're so caught up in taking care of other people, making sure strangers have the most tranquil beach holiday of their lives, that they can't spend time with their own family! I was sure they'd have given it up long ago."

Her mother had sat mute through his tirade, one elbow resting on the car windowsill, her hand pressed to tight lips, an unfolded map occupying her lap. They'd been studying it earlier, looking for things to do on their holiday.

"And…" her father had continued, "do you know what she said when I asked her about it? She said they couldn't leave the inn for long anymore, because it couldn't run without them and was getting busier every year, that it was time for us to make the trip. Can you believe it? I mean, when I pointed out that retirement was supposed to involve relaxation, maybe a trip to Europe, she laughed and said, 'To each their own, my darling boy.'"

He'd huffed in frustration then and pointed out that the map they were using didn't have the road the inn was on. "What kind of place isn't on the map?"

Kate remembered being quietly fascinated by her own grandmother then. Her father was right, she hardly knew either of her grandparents, since she often only saw them once or twice a year. And every time had been either at their home in Sydney, or at a campground halfway between the two locations in Scott's Head on the verge of a long, horse-shoe beach with soft rolling waves.

She loved the idea of moving to a remote beach as they had, to a place that didn't show up on the map and starting a new life. A life that didn't involve stop and go traffic, private school, or boys that pushed you over in the playground and laughed when you grazed your knees.

Instead they could live in a mysterious inn that wasn't on the map, along a road with not a single car anywhere in sight, fringed by waves. That kind of life would be fine by her.

And that was her first memory of admiration for Nan. There had been so many times since that she'd lost track, and at some point, she'd begun to take her grandmother for granted, assumed she'd always be there, and stopped wondering, stopped being fascinated by the details of her out-of-the-ordinary life. She was just Nan. The woman who baked the most delicious cinnamon tea cake in the state, or the most scrumptious scones. The woman who loved to sing to her chooks while she scattered seed on the ground for them to peck at. And the woman who loved the ocean almost as much as she loved her granddaughters. Almost, she'd always remind them with a wink, but not quite.

Kate's eyes misted and she wiped them with a quick movement, peering through the tears to find the road's uneven edges and make sure to keep her car firmly between them.

Her mother had made some comment then. Something wise in her kind, patient voice. Something that'd soothed her father's nerves and made him smile, wiped the anxious lines from his face. She'd always done that. Been able to smooth his uneven edges. Then she'd turned to look back at her three girls, wedged side by side into the back seat of the car, smiled and patted their knees one by one. She didn't have to say anything. Kate knew what it meant. She'd had a special way of making Kate feel as though everything was all right. So many years later, she hadn't felt that way in a long time.

* * *

THE CR-V's tires slipped and skidded as she pulled the car into the inn's driveway. She'd almost missed the turn, distracted by a possum's last-minute twilight dash across the road. She pulled the car onto the verge, her breathing ragged. A cloud of dust swept over the car, enveloping it like smoke from a campfire, the headlights dimming in its midst.

Kate's eyes squeezed shut a moment and she exhaled with slow deliberation. An image of the startled possum barely escaping her tires flashed across her mind's eye. She shuddered. Just as her heart rate was about to return to normal, a thud on the car's bonnet sent a bolt of adrenaline through her body.

In the dim dusk light, she saw a familiar face. Jack, the handyman who'd worked at the inn for almost as long as she could remember and who had to be at least seventy years old, grinned at her from beneath a worn, tan Akubra hat. Behind him, a lop-sided timber sign painted in a gaudy dark pink announced *The Waratah Inn, Beachside Bed and Breakfast.*

She pushed the car door open with a smile. "You scared the life out of me."

He chuckled, then stepped forward with open arms to embrace her. She wrapped her arms around his waist, enjoying the familiar scent of fresh cut timber, leather, and Old Spice.

Her memory flashed back to another time. Jack had taught her to ride. The horse's name was Janet. She'd laughed about that at the time and asked him what kind of person called a horse Janet. He'd told her it was as good a name as any for a horse, and besides, didn't she look like a Janet?

He'd held the reins while she and Janet walked around the yard. Then he'd shown her how to hold on with her legs and use pressure from her heels to urge the horse forward. Finally, he'd given her a lesson on how to hold the reins in her hands, loose but firm enough to be able to communicate with the animal about where she wanted to go and when she wanted to slow down or stop.

That had been a good day during a time when good days were few and far between. After the accident, Nan had remained in her downstairs bedroom for weeks, unwilling to come out and face the world. Mima and Jack had been the ones who'd comforted Kate and her sisters, taken them to town to buy groceries, watched as they swam or ducked waves, and helped them buy the school uniforms they'd need to start attending the new school.

When Jack brought Janet up to the inn, Kate had been sitting on the verandah, staring off into the distance, thinking about all the things she missed. All the things she'd never have. She'd smiled at the sight of the horse, then felt immediate guilt over that smile, wiping it away and replacing it with a scowl. He'd pretended not to notice, and patted Janet's long, brown neck instead.

"Isn't she a beauty? I was hoping you might help me with her. She needs someone to take care of her, and I'm so busy with everything around here…"

She hadn't needed a second invitation. With a few bounds she was down the stairs and standing beside the bay horse, her hand pressed to the animal's fine fur coat.

"She's so soft," she'd said. "What's her name?"

Jack had been the one to help her onto Janet's back, and ever since, she'd loved horseback riding. It was an escape, an adventure. And she'd be forever grateful to him for introducing in her a love of the majestic animals.

He faced her now with a smile, his eyes gleaming. "Good to see you, love. I hope the drive wasn't too bad." He shifted his hat back with the tip of one finger.

She shook her head. "It was horrible, but it's over now. I'm glad to finally be here."

"Let me help with your luggage."

"I should move the car, I'm in the way here," she said, scanning the winding gravel driveway that encircled the inn's front yard.

"I'll help you inside then move the car to the parking lot for you."

"Thank you, Jack."

He patted her on the back, an awkward but sweet gesture that made her throat smart.

"You're welcome, hon. I'm glad you're here. We've missed you."

Jack was a fixture at the Waratah Inn. He repaired anything that needed it, and Nan counted on him to help her keep the place running. Generally, he kept to himself and barely uttered a word to anyone. These few words of greeting were the most he'd said to Kate in years, and they meant a lot.

She couldn't speak as a wave of sorrow washed over her. She'd been gone too long. Nan had asked her to visit, maybe she'd even suspected she was sick but hadn't wanted to say anything. Now Kate would never know, and she wouldn't see Nan's smiling face or bouncing grey curls as they marched along the sand together, arm in arm, ever again.

She slung her handbag over one shoulder and stopped to stare at the inn. Peeling pink paint with white trim. The verandahs that encircled the first and second floors were lit up with the soft glow of lamplight. Inside, a couple of the rooms were lit as well, but the rest of the regal old building had fallen into darkness.

With a grunt, Jack slung her suitcase up onto one shoulder and marched to the inn. Her brow furrowed. The man was a machine. There was no slowing him down. He carried her suitcase as though it weighed nothing, boasting the physique of a much younger man.

She hurried after him, with one worried glance back at the CR-V. Its headlights illuminated the driveway, the boot door hung wide open and the bell dinged in a perfect rhythm to let her know the keys were in the ignition. Still, she couldn't think straight. The inn was drawing her to itself, like a bee to honey. She had to touch its weathered timber, feel the hard, cool boards beneath her feet, see the rooms that held so many memories and so much of her heart.

As she climbed the first few steps, her pulse quickened. Nan wasn't there to greet her at the door. She remembered a similar feeling when Pop died. She'd been eleven years old at the time and came to Cabarita with her family for the funeral. She'd ascended this same set of steps to find only Nan inside waiting for them in the large, high-ceilinged sitting room. The room had felt empty and Nan looked shrivelled, seated in the large, leather wing-backed armchair. She'd realised her grandmother was getting old. That was seventeen years ago.

She paused at the top of the staircase and inhaled a deep breath. The screen door slapped shut behind Jack and he disappeared into the inn, taking her suitcase with him.

How could she stay here without Nan? The Waratah Inn was Nan, it shouldn't exist with her gone.

The door flew open, and two lined hands stretched to meet her.

"Kate! Sweetheart! You made it. Come on inside and I'll make you a cup of tea. You must be freezing!"

Kate accepted the embrace Mima offered, almost getting smothered in the process by the woman's ample bosoms and purple knit cardigan. Only in Cabarita would someone define a balmy twenty degrees Celsius as freezing. Her eyes filled with tears, and she smiled as Mima patted her back and kissed her cheek.

"I'm fine, thanks Mima. It's good to see you too. Tea would be lovely."

Mima bustled her into the kitchen, pulled up a stool for her to sit on, and set about boiling the kettle, all the while regaling her with a moment by moment account of her day. The woman's wide hips swayed with each step. Her salt and pepper curls were pulled into a bun on top of her head but couldn't be tamed, instead tumbling down on each side of her face. Her blue eyes sparkled as she spoke.

"We've still got two guests. Can you believe it? They know what's going on, and yet they stay. The other couple that were here checked out right away, after giving their sympathies, but this couple. Wowsers!"

Mima set two mugs on the bench. "So, I guess we'll shut the place down for a while as soon as they leave. But that's something we can discuss later."

She pulled a teapot from the overhead cupboard and measured a tablespoon of tea leaves into the pot. Then, filled it with boiling hot water. "And do you know, I was in the breakfast nook this morning, reading my Home and Garden magazine... I get one every month dear, I know it's pointless since I live at the inn these days and don't really have my own home or garden, but I like the decorating tips and I always thought that maybe one day my cooking might earn me a featured article."

She set the lid on the pot, turned it to the right, then to the left, resting her hand on top of the pot while she continued. "But that's neither here nor there, you don't want to hear about the silly dreams of an old woman. Now, where was I? Oh yes, the lizard…"

"Lizard?" Kate gave her a confused look. Mima's tales were famously long and winding.

"Yes, the lizard! It came creeping into the breakfast nook. I don't know where exactly it came from. It was one of those blue-tongued ones, you know? And it scared me half to death because when you see the head, it looks like a black snake. It's not until the tiny little legs come into view that you can breathe again.

"So, I thought we had a black snake, and a pretty big one at that, in the breakfast nook. And of course, I don't eat my breakfast until after everyone else has finished and gone about their day. So, I was all by myself. I didn't scream, mind, I gasped. Because, after all, it's not my first run-in with a snake. They're common enough around here. But I tell you, I was relieved to see those little legs when it pushed past the chair it was hiding behind.

"I like to sit in the breakfast nook to eat my breakfast, and usually Edie… uh… your Nan, would come join me after she'd finished her morning walk. We'd sit there together every day and have a cup of coffee and talk about everything going on in our lives. She'd do the crossword, and I'd do my knitting. So, I knew something was up this morning when that lizard came in, and once my heart had recovered, I looked down at my watch… and Edie wasn't there. That's when I went looking for her and found her on the path that leads down to the cove. Oh dear, I've made you cry. I'm sorry, love. And now I'm crying too. I can't help it you know, I'm a sympathetic crier. If I see tears, I join in. It's the way I am."

Kate let the tears fall. She hadn't cried more than a few tears since she'd heard the news about Nan's passing, and the pain in Mima's voice was more than she could withstand.

"It's okay. I'm fine. I hope she didn't suffer..." She sniffled into her jacket sleeve.

Mima set down the teapot and waddled to where Kate sat, and embraced her all over again. Tears streaked the old woman's face and her bottom lip wobbled before she crushed Kate's head to her chest. "No sweetheart, I don't believe she did. She looked as peaceful as can be."

Finally, Mima released her hold on Kate.

The inn felt like a part of her. She didn't visit often enough these days, and with Mima and Jack sitting in this sturdy old kitchen, she was at home, loved. She scanned the room, her eyes misty, taking it all in as an ache filled her heart. Peeling white paint, an ancient steel stovetop, and racks of drying herbs hung with string beside silver pots and pans with blackened bottoms.

This kitchen stirred up memories of hot chocolate with tiny marshmallows, bacon and eggs with toast, and soft hugs that smelled like woodsmoke and chocolate chip biscuits.

"It's good to be home," she said.

Mima poured tea into two mismatched, floral print china cups with a smile. "You're home, sweetheart, and even though there's grief in my heart, I've a bubble of joy working its way up in there for seeing you."

KATE SAT at the vintage dressing table and spun slowly on the chair. The room Mima had led her to after their cup of tea was the same one she and her sisters had shared as young girls. Only now, it was decorated as a guest room.

A single queen-sized bed with an outdated, floral bedspread squatted in the middle of the room. Dark, antique side tables sat on either side of the bed, one with a blue lamp, one without.

The rug beneath the bed was worn but looked to have once been a shade of pale blue. On another table by the window, a small bowl held an assortment of seashells and sun-bleached coral. Beside it, a cream coloured vase was filled with fresh cut flowers, no doubt from Nan's beloved garden.

As a girl, whenever she couldn't find Nan, she knew to run to the long, rectangular garden out the back. She'd find Nan there, dressed in a pair of denim overalls, with an old straw hat perched on top of her head, wispy, every-which-way hair flying out beneath the brim. She'd wear yellow gloves and carry a pair of secateurs or a small shovel in one hand. Her boots would be caked with dirt, and she'd always say, "Damn this sandy soil, it's so hard to grow anything." Then she'd smile and wave Kate in through the rickety gate that guarded the rows of vegetables, flowers, and seedling plants from the rabbits and possums.

"Come on in love, you can help me figure out how to make these waratahs grow." Then Kate would pull on a second pair of gloves, much too large for her small hands, and together they'd spread fertiliser, or lovingly trim Nan's waratah shrubs.

Kate sighed and walked to the window. She fingered a piece of coral in the bowl and stared out through the second-story window and into the darkness. She could make out the familiar outline of the garden shed, and beside it the chook pen. The garden was there too, though she couldn't make out much other than a shadowy fence and the tops of a few bushy plants.

A scratching sound overhead caught her ear and she frowned at the ceiling. Did they have rats in the inn? Then, the scratching turned to a gnawing and her stomach clenched. Something was eating the building from the inside out. Waves sighed, crashed onto the sandy shores of the nearby beach, drowning out the soft shuffling overhead bringing a sense of peace to her soul.

She was fifteen and living at the inn when the rhythm of waves first soothed her nerves. The funeral had passed in a blur, and life had returned to some semblance of normality, though Nan still kept to her bedroom. She, Bindi, and Reeda were crammed into this room with one set of bunk beds and a single for Reeda by the window. Kate had been grateful at the time that the inn was so busy they all had to live together in one room. They clung to each other in those days as though letting go might mean never seeing each other again.

Kate rested a hand on the windowsill and strained her eyes in the direction of the cove. The path that led down to the sand was there, a little overgrown, but she could make it out in the moonlight. Then, it was obscured by undergrowth and bushes. She knew beyond lay the dunes. Rising mounds of sand where she and her sisters had spent countless hours, pretending to be princesses from far off lands and rescuing each other from unnamed monsters, or imagining they were jillaroos, rounding up a herd of wild brumbies and bringing them home to break and train until they ate from the girls' hands, nuzzling their open palms softly with whiskered snouts.

Kate shook her head and turned away from the window. Those days were such distant memories now, like whispers of a time past that would never come again. Whispers that couldn't be caught, and if she grasped too hard at the memories, they'd disappear like a vapour.

When was the last time she'd seen Nyreeda? Her older sister hadn't come up from Sydney for Christmas. She'd been busy. At least that was what she'd told Nan and Nan hadn't seemed inclined to be pushed on the subject.

"Your sister has enough to deal with," was all she'd say, and when Kate asked what she meant by that, she'd simply smile. "We all have our own stuff, my love. That's why it's important to show people compassion even when you don't understand why they do what they do."

The memory caught Kate off guard. What had Nan been referring to? From all she knew, Reeda was a highly successful interior designer with her own business in Sydney. Her services were in demand with the upwardly mobile elite of the northern beaches. And she was married to a handsome surgeon who, from what Kate had seen, seemed to adore her.

What "stuff" had Nan been referring to? And why wouldn't Reeda talk to Kate about it herself? She knew the answer to that one at least. Reeda didn't talk to her about anything, not anymore. They'd all but lost touch over the past five years, and if not for Nan, may not have seen each other at all.

And there was Bindi, who seemed lost in a world of her own. She'd been there with them at Christmas, at least physically, but she'd been quieter than usual, and spent a lot of time on her own at the beach.

Why did the passing years have to mean that relationships changed? They'd been so close as girls, and yet from the first day after Reeda left for University, those bonds had stretched, then frayed, and finally snapped one Christmas about five years earlier when the three of them had a blow up over something trivial. She couldn't remember what it was that'd started the argument, only that they'd all yelled things at each other, and she'd said things she wished she could take back.

When it was her turn to graduate from Kingscliff Public High School, she'd been so focused on getting away from Cabarita Beach and starting a new life, she hadn't taken the time to think about the fact that nothing would ever be the same again. She could never return to that life — a life of peaceful warmth, with Nan cooking scrambled eggs over the ancient stove top when she padded down the stairs in her pyjamas. Or sitting in her rocking chair, knitting, and glancing at Kate over the top of half-circle black rimmed glasses, as Kate read out her homework, nodding every now and then to something she'd said.

Kate's throat tightened, and a lump filled it so that it was hard to breathe. Why couldn't she have appreciated everything then? Now it was too late.

CHAPTER 4

AUGUST 1995

CABARITA BEACH

*K*ate plodded down the wide staircase, her slippers slick on the hardwood boards. She'd slept late. She hadn't been able to get to sleep until well after three a.m. Anxiety over all the tasks that lay ahead had kept her awake, thinking through lists of to-dos and questions, like what are we going to do with the inn now? And if we sell it, what will happen to Mima and Jack? Not to mention the horses, the chooks, and the cat that showed up from time to time and drank milk from one of Mima's saucers without Nan knowing about it, since she'd be darned if she'd take on a cat as well as everything else she was managing.

Though of course, Kate had seen Nan feeding the cat herself often enough and checking over her shoulder to make sure Mima didn't catch her.

She chuckled at the memory, then pushed the birds nest her hair had become with all her tossing and turning, out of her eyes. In the kitchen, she made a beeline for the espresso machine. A luxury they didn't need and couldn't afford, according to Mima, but something Nan had insisted on buying. The two of them had argued over the purchase innumerable times, until finally Nan had said it was for the guests, and that was that.

Kate and Nan had enjoyed many a cup of hot, steaming coffee together whenever she visited. Nan always said, coffee was for the mornings when you couldn't rub the sheet marks off your face. And that was how Kate felt. Her eyes were half-lidded, her body felt heavy, and her head thudded with sinus pressure. She hoped she wasn't coming down with anything. That was the last thing she needed. Right now, a clear head, logical thinking, was the best thing.

Someone had to organise a funeral. She assumed the task would probably fall to her, unless her sisters materialised sometime soon. Then, perhaps they could do it together, if they didn't kill each other in the process.

She poured coffee into a large mug, then cozied up to the bench, feet resting on the bottom rung of the stool, to sip it gingerly.

The kitchen phone rested in its cradle just above her head. She eyed it with a stab of guilt. She hadn't given a single thought to her fiancé since she arrived at the inn. She should at least try to call him and tell him she'd made it there safely. He was probably worried about her. Though she couldn't be sure, since she'd never seen that particular emotion in him. It didn't really match his dark, tailored suits, perfectly coiffed hair, and chiselled features. When she pictured Davis in her mind, it surprised her all over again that he'd chosen her. Men like Davis, the Chief Technology Officer for a large, lifestyle company in downtown Brisbane, usually chose women who wore designer gowns with décolletage fighting to burst free from the neckline, and diamonds glimmering on various parts of their body.

That just wasn't her. She usually wore her chef's jacket, black and white chequered pants, Doc Marten boots, and her hair pulled back into a messy bun on top of her head with a hairnet holding the whole thing in place. Her look didn't exactly prompt the word "glamour" to come to mind. And yet, he'd asked her out after they met outside one of the corporate functions she'd been asked to cook for, and he'd attended as a guest. He'd been smoking on the balcony, and she'd been looking for a breath of fresh air at the end of a long night. She'd quipped about the health benefits of fresh air, he'd laughed, and the chemistry between them had ignited.

Still, she couldn't help wondering sometimes if perhaps he deserved someone else. Someone who fit him in all the ways she didn't. They were supposed to be getting married, but she'd postponed the wedding date three times. She said it was because they were both so busy, but when he hadn't seemed to mind, she wondered if perhaps her fears that they weren't suited to one another had some kind of merit.

She tugged the phone from its cradle and punched in his office number. Pressing the receiver to her ear, she waited, drumming her fingers against the bench top. The phone rang out, and she hit redial to try again.

This time, he answered. "Yyyello."

She smiled. "Hey, it's me."

His voice softened. "Kate, I was wondering when you were going to call. How'd you go?"

"I got here late last night. The traffic was horrendous. But everything's fine. Reeda and Bindi aren't here yet, so it's me, Mima, Jack and two guests who haven't found the good sense to check out yet for some reason." She scrubbed a hand over her face.

He chuckled. "You should kick them out."

"I don't think Nan would want us to, but I might if they

don't leave soon." She groaned. "And now I have to think about funerals, and plans for the inn, and all kinds of things I don't want to think about."

"Won't you sell the place?" he asked.

She grimaced. "I'm sure we will. I don't see how we can keep it running. That is, if she's left it to us girls. We haven't seen the solicitor yet about her will, so there's really no point thinking about things like that. Knowing Nan, she probably left the place to Mima and Jack. And honestly, that would be fine with me. If I don't have to take responsibility for figuring out what to do with it, then I can simply organise the funeral, say goodbye and go back to my life in Brisbane. And back to you, back to normal."

His voice sounded more distant. "Look, hon, I have to go. Work is crazy right now and I've got a million things to do. I'm sure you'll work it all out."

"We'll probably have the funeral next week. Do you think you can make it down?" Kate took another sip of coffee and scalded the end of her tongue. She gasped, then blew on her tongue as best she could, setting the mug back on the bench.

"Ahhh… I'm not sure. As I said, we've got a lot going on, and I really have to be here for it, since I'm the boss. Pick a day, let me know, and I'll see what I can do. Okay?"

Her brow furrowed and she chewed the inside of one cheek. He knew how much Nan meant to her. She was basically Kate's parent, the only one she had left anyway. "Okay."

"Look, I'll call you later, hon. Love you."

He'd hung up before the words "Love you," had left her mouth in response. Her eyes narrowed, and she stared at the receiver a moment before pushing it back into its place on the wall.

Footsteps echoed in the living room, then Mima rounded the corner and into the kitchen.

"Ah, there you are! Good morning, sweetheart, I hope you slept well."

She shook her head with a glum smile. "Nope. But I have coffee." She raised her mug as though in salute.

Mima rolled her eyes. "You and Nan with that coffee! Pfft! A good cup of tea is what you need. Coffee clogs your arteries."

Kate bit down on her lip to keep from laughing. Mima always railed against the evils of coffee. That and surfing. She couldn't understand why anyone would stand on a flimsy board and trust a wave to carry them to shore when God gave them a set of perfectly good feet and land to stand on.

"Are you hungry? I made a batch of scones, and they're cool enough to eat. Your Nan's recipe." Mima pulled a dish-cloth from a tray of soft, golden-topped scones, cooling on a rack.

"Um... I haven't eaten breakfast yet so maybe I shouldn't."

"Good Lord, rules are for fools, my girl. Eat what you want, when you want. That's what I say." She giggled, as she patted her rotund rear end. "Perhaps I've found the source of the problem," she whispered, then laughed out loud as she refilled the kettle from the tap.

Kate laughed with her. "No, you're right. I don't have to follow the rules, I can be flexible, footloose and fancy-free..."

Mima flicked the switch on the kettle with a chortle. "Uh-huh. Sure you can, sweetheart."

"No, I can. Let's do it. Scones for breakfast. I'm breaking all the rules today. I slept late and now I'm eating scones with jam and cream for breakfast. Who knows, next I might go upstairs and mess up all the books on the bookshelf so they're out of order."

Mima waved her arms over her head. "Hallelujah! It's a miracle!" She laughed as she put scones onto a plate. "Let's go to the breakfast nook. It's so nice in there this time of day."

* * *

SUNLIGHT FILTERED through the plantation shutters casting dancing prisms of light over the pale blue seat cushions and making the painted white timber furniture look new again.

On closer inspection, Kate could see the cracks in the paint and the dark smudges of mould and grime growing in out-of-reach places beneath table tops, close to the bottom of table legs, and in between the black and white tiles that covered the narrow floor in the breakfast nook. It'd once been a covered porch off the back of the Waratah Inn, and had since been enclosed when Nan decided it would be the best place to sit in the morning to have her coffee and ruminate over the early morning's activities and what was to come.

Nan always considered the inn her home and the staff who worked there her family. When guests came to stay, they were invited unceremoniously and with great affection into the family for the duration of their trip. Nan and Pop had decided early on that the inn was their retirement plan and treated it accordingly. They worked hard in the early hours of the day, rested until evening, then set to work again to make their guests comfortable. All the hours in between were for them to relax and enjoy themselves in what they called their little corner of paradise.

Kate had asked Nan once, only a few years earlier, why they didn't close up the inn for guests when they hit retirement age. They could've lived a quiet life, Pop throwing out his fishing line in the cove, Nan walking on the beach or puttering in her garden. Why bother waiting on guests. She'd told Kate it was their dream, their crazy little dream. No one understood it but them, they never had. And what would she do with her days if she had no work to do? She'd go stir crazy sitting around with no one but Pop to talk to. Much as she loved him, she'd added with a wink.

Kate sat in one of the chairs across from Mima, who lowered herself with a huff of air and a grunt into her own. She smoothed back the grey hair that was pulled into a tight little bun at the nape of her neck. Wisps and tendrils had escaped and were flying free around her face in loose curls, the grey streaked with more white than Kate remembered from Christmas.

Between them sat two cups of tea on matching saucers, and a plate of warm, soft scones, with side dishes of cream and strawberry jam.

"Made from the strawberries Edie picked in her garden in autumn," Mima said as she pushed a spoon into the chunky jam. "So, how are things with that handsome man of yours?"

Mima sliced open one of the scones.

"Things are good, I think. I mean, we've postponed the wedding again; we're both so busy."

Mima didn't say a word, just smeared jam on her scone.

"We'll get there, we have to be sure the timing is right," added Kate.

Mima nodded. "You do what you feel's right to do. But can I ask you something?"

"Okay." Kate wasn't sure she wanted to hear whatever it was Mima had to say.

"When it's right, you know it is. You don't have to wonder or wait for the right time. If he's the man for you, you'll be tripping over your own feet trying so hard to get to that altar."

Kate dropped a dollop of cream on her own scone, irritation boiling up from within. It wasn't anything she hadn't thought before. But hearing it come from Mima's lips didn't help her feel any better about it, and she bit back a defensive retort.

Mima had been single for as long as Kate had known her, and as far as she knew, had never married. What did she really know about love?

"He's the right man for me. We're busy. That's all it is."

Mima smiled. "Of course he is. And the two of you will be the most beautiful couple around. Him with his dark hair and suave suits, and you with those big green eyes and killer figure."

"I have a killer figure? Hardly." Kate rolled her eyes as she bit into the scone. It practically melted in her mouth.

"Please, sweetheart. Enjoy what God gave you because Heaven only knows it doesn't stay that way forever. You're beautiful, and you should know that. We women waste far too much of our youth wishing it away, envying everyone around us, and before we have a chance to stop and enjoy our freedom, our looks, our energy and strength, time has ripped it all away." Mima shook her head. "Don't spend your young years wishing, sweetheart. Enjoy them."

Kate nodded. "You're so right. I'll try to, I promise. And by the way, these scones are amazing. I could eat a dozen of them."

"Well, don't stop on my account. I can always make more. And you're practically skin and bone."

Kate laughed. "Thanks, Mima. Hey, I was wondering — do you know what Nan wanted, what her final wishes were?" This was an awkward conversation to have. Mima and Jack lived at the inn, but Kate still didn't know what Nan had decided to do with it, if she'd decided anything at all. Looking back, she realised they should've had a discussion about it years ago, but none of them had imagined Nan would leave them so soon. She'd always been so youthful, strong, and vibrant.

Mima's brow furrowed and she tapped one cheek with a finger bent by arthritis. "Let me see, I know she wrote a will, because Jack and I witnessed her signing it. She has a solic-itor somewhere in Kingscliff, I've probably got his number in the rolodex back there in the office. I didn't get to read the will, mind you. So, I can't tell you what's in it. But I know there's a copy around here somewhere, and some other things she wrote down for you girls as well."

"What about funeral arrangements; did she have anything to say about that, do you remember?"

Mima smiled, her full lips pulling so wide that her eyes almost disappeared beneath her wrinkles. "Now, that I *do* know. She wanted us to have it in the cove and sprinkle her ashes in the waves. She was pretty clear about that."

Kate nodded, her throat tight. "That makes sense."

A tap on the door frame caught Kate's attention and she swivelled in place.

"Anyone home?" called a familiar voice.

Mima lurched to her feet, her eyes lighting up. "Bindi! You made it, honey. Oh, just look at you."

Mima embraced Bindi, pressing her sister's head into her bosom the way she did with anyone she hugged. Bindi's wispy sandy-blonde hair was pulled into a ponytail and sagged beneath Mima's hug. Bindi wore a pair of jeans, a long-sleeved flannel shirt and a pair of chunky boots. Her green eyes looked tired and freckles stood out across her pale nose and cheeks.

Kate stood slowly, brushing scone crumbs from her lap as she did. Her heart thudded. Bindi had always been good to her, but she'd never been one to keep in contact much. It was hard to stay in touch when you worked nights, weekends, and everything in between as a chef. People counted on her, and for the past decade everything and everyone else in her life had come in second best. Guilt washed over her as she took in the sight of her youngest sister's tired face. She didn't know anything about her — what was she doing, was she in love, healthy or sick, happy or sad?

"Hi Bindi, it's good to see you." She offered open arms and Bindi stepped into them.

With an awkward pat to her sister's back, she smiled. "How was the flight from Melbourne?"

Bindi shrugged. "It was fine. You're looking good."

"Thank you. You too."

When had things become so stilted between them? They used to be able to talk about anything, laughing together until their sides hurt. If she remembered rightly, there'd been a time Bindi had peed her pants when they were playing tennis one evening and laughing over some nonsense or other, unable to stop. They'd had the kind of connection other sisters envied. And now they were behaving like strangers.

"I'm going to take my bags upstairs and grab a shower, if that's okay, Mima. I'm pretty tired." Bindi ran a hand over her eyes, and Kate studied her. She looked tired. Something was going on with her little sister. Or maybe this was how she was these days.

Mima excused herself to walk Bindi up to her bedroom. Kate slumped into her chair and picked up the scone. She took another bite, then set the pastry back on the plate, her appetite gone. Sadness balled like a fist in her chest.

Without Nan, she was all alone in the world.

"Helloooo!" called a voice from the reception area.

Kate hurried to greet whoever it was, and to tell them the inn was closed to new bookings. With Mima busy upstairs, and Jack out doing who knew what somewhere on the property, she was the only one available to meet an unexpected guest. She glanced down at her pyjamas in dismay and smoothed her flyaway hair back as best she could. She pushed out her chest and stepped through the arched doorway that lead from the sitting room.

"Good morning, I'm sorry to say that the inn isn't open to new bookings…"

A woman stood in the reception area, her back to Kate. She wore a narrow grey pencil skirt that hugged her lithe figure, offset by a pink knit jumper. Long, straight hair swung like a waterfall with each movement. Perfectly manicured hands pressed to her narrow hips and she spun about on stiletto heels to face Kate with a smile. A thick blunt fringe that brushed against her eyelashes, almost entirely obscured her eyebrows but accentuated wide, brown eyes

"Kate, how lovely to see you. You look… nice." Nyreeda's gaze swept up and down Kate.

"Reeda, wow, we weren't expecting you yet. I'm sorry, I literally just woke up… rough night." Kate kissed her eldest sister's cheek, then stood back to study her.

"You look like you stepped off a runway, and not the airport kind," said Kate, cocking her head to one side.

"Thanks. Where is everyone?"

"I don't know where Jack is, in fact I'm surprised he didn't meet you at the gate. He was hovering close by when I glanced outside earlier. Bindi arrived a few minutes before you, so Mima's showing her upstairs. You must've missed her at the airport by a hair. I'm sure she'll be down soon."

"Bindi's here? Great, I guess we're all here, then." Reeda drummed her fingers against her hips.

"Want me to walk you upstairs? I'm actually not sure which room Mima has you staying in, but she can tell us that." Kate crossed her arms over her chest, painfully aware of the contrast between her fashion model sister and the vagabond look she was currently sporting.

"Thanks. It's so strange to be back here. Isn't it?" Reeda scanned the room, her eyes softening. "And Nan's not here."

The last was almost in a whisper, so that Kate couldn't be entirely sure she'd heard the words.

Kate inhaled sharply as another stab of grief hit her unexpectedly. It came in waves. If she forgot Nan was gone for a moment, the realisation crushed her anew each time it hit her.

"Yeah, I know. Really strange." She pursed her lips. "Come on, let's go upstairs and find Mima."

* * *

KATE PEEKED INTO THE SMALL, untidy office that was wedged behind the inn's kitchen and beside the tacked-on laundry. It felt strange to pry in Nan's office; it'd always been the place she'd come to sit with Nan while she ran over the bookwork, her black-rimmed glasses perched on the end of her button nose.

Where would Nan have kept her will?

A small, rusted filing cabinet was pushed up against the wall behind a worn timber desk. That was a good place to start looking.

She squeezed in behind the desk and sat in the swivel chair, since there wasn't room to do anything else. After a few minutes of rifling through files, she still hadn't found anything. She sighed and spun around in the chair to face the desk, massaging her temples with her fingertips. The beginnings of a headache had set in, and she suspected it had something to do with her sisters' arrival. Tensions between the three of them ran high these days, and none seemed able to shrug things off the way they had in the past.

An old-fashioned black rotary phone sat on the desk and she eyed it. She really should call Marco, find out how things were going with the new menu. She'd been dreading making the phone call, since she'd abandoned them right when the restaurant was rolling out a menu she'd designed. Marco had put his faith in her after so many years of tightly controlling every aspect of his restaurant. She'd been so excited to show him what she could do. Now that might never happen.

She dialled the restaurant's number, her anxiety growing with each ring. After a minute of ringing, one of the kitchen staff finally answered. She asked for Marco, then sat chewing a fingernail while she waited for the call to be transferred to his office.

She could see him, seated behind his large, hardwood desk, hunched down in his expensive ergonomic chair, his small, black eyes fixed on the computer screen in front of him. He'd mutter over the figures he was collating, about how many guests had attended the restaurant the night before, what the takings were, tips distributed, staff numbers and everything else. His business ran like clockwork, and he knew every last detail about it, down to how many napkins were used and needed laundering. He was the most fastidious restaurant manager she'd ever worked with, and his tight control over every detail of the business made it a challenge to work with him, especially when it came to creative risk taking.

"Hello?"

"Hi Marco, it's Kate."

"Kate, I hope your trip is okay. I know how hard family funerals can be."

She nodded. "Thanks Marco. Actually, I was calling to see how the new menu worked out and to tell you again how sorry I am that I couldn't be there for the first night."

He hesitated and she could hear the rustle of papers. "It didn't go well, Kate. I'm sorry to say it, but I've had to roll back to the old menu."

Her mouth fell open. "But…"

"It was a complete disaster, Kate. The kitchen staff

couldn't pull it off without you, and we had more complaints than ever from customers. The scallops were overcooked, the salmon undercooked, there was too much soy sauce on the crab... you name it, they got it wrong. We needed you here, Kate."

She squeezed her eyes shut and pinched the bridge of her nose with two fingertips. "I'm sorry, Marco. I wanted to be there."

"I know, and I get why you couldn't be. But you have to understand, this is my business, my livelihood, and I can't risk it for a new menu that my staff can't deliver. I thought it was a good menu, and perhaps one day we can try it again with you at the helm, but it didn't work. Not this time."

She scrubbed a hand over her face. This couldn't be happening. "I'm really sorry to hear that Marco."

"So, can we expect to see you here on Monday?" His voice was gruff.

She could feel the tension pinching a nerve in her neck, and the headache that'd been building in the base of her skull reverberated through to her forehead. "Um... not Monday. I'm going to need to take a bit more time off. We've still got to arrange the funeral, and I'll have some loose ends to tie up. We don't know what Nan wanted to do with the inn yet, so I'll have to meet with her solicitor, then figure out a way forward."

He wasn't going to like it, but there wasn't much she could do about it. She hadn't prioritised Nan the way she should've while her grandmother was alive. She certainly wasn't going to make the same mistake after her death. The least she could do was to give Nan's final wishes her full attention.

"I see, well you know I need a chef in my kitchen, Kate. So, I'm going to have to put you on unpaid leave so I can hire a temporary replacement."

Her breath caught in her throat. "It's only for a week or two, Marco."

"That's fine, Kate. Take the time you need, but I have to replace you, the kitchen can't keep operating without someone in charge. I've been stepping in, but it's been a long time since I managed a kitchen and I'm a bit rusty. I need a pro in there."

She nodded silently, her eyes blinking. "I understand."

"Give me a call when you're ready to come back," he said.

When he hung up the phone, Kate lowered her pounding head onto the cool desk. After five years of loyal service, she'd expected more from Marco. Though knowing him as well as she did, she knew she shouldn't have. He was as cutthroat in business as he was pedantic. She'd never seen him show an ounce of sentimentality, why would she think he'd start now?

KEEP READING "THE WARATAH INN"

ALSO BY LILLY MIRREN

The Summer Sisters

Set against the golden sands and crystal clear waters of Cabarita Beach three sisters inherit an inn and discover a mystery about their grandmother's past that changes everything they thought they knew about their family...

Christmas at The Waratah Inn

Liz Cranwell is divorced and alone at Christmas. When her friends convince her to holiday at The Waratah Inn, she's dreading her first Christmas on her own. Instead she discovers that strangers can be the balm to heal the wounds of a lonely heart in this heartwarming Christmas story.

EMERALD COVE SERIES

Cottage on Oceanview Lane

When a renowned book editor returns to her roots, she rediscovers her strength & her passion in this heartwarming novel.

Seaside Manor Bed & Breakfast

The Seaside Manor Bed and Breakfast has been an institution in Emerald Cove for as long as anyone can remember. But things are changing and Diana is nervous about what the future might hold for her and her husband, not to mention the historic business.

Bungalow on Pelican Way

Moving to the Cove gave Rebecca De Vries a place to hide from her abusive ex. Now that he's in jail, she can get back to living her life as a police officer in her adopted hometown working alongside her intractable but very attractive boss, Franklin.

Chalet on Cliffside Drive

At forty-four years of age, Ben Silver thought he'd never find love. When he moves to Emerald Cove, he does it to support his birth mother, Diana, after her husband's sudden death. But then he meets Vicky.

Christmas in Emerald Cove

The Flannigan family has been through a lot together. They've grown and changed over the years and now have a blended and extended family that doesn't always see eye to eye. But this Christmas they'll learn that love can overcome all of the pain and differences of the past in this inspiring Christmas tale.

HOME SWEET HOME SERIES

Home Sweet Home

Trina is starting over after a painful separation from her husband of almost twenty years. Grief and loss force her to return to her hometown where she has to deal with all of the things she left behind to rebuild her life, piece by piece; a hometown she hasn't visited since high school graduation.

No Place Like Home

Lisa never thought she'd leave her high-profile finance job in the city to work in a small-town bakery. She also never expected to still be single in her forties.

GLOSSARY OF TERMS

Dear reader,

Since this book is set in Australia there may be some terms you're not familiar with. I've included them below to help you out! I hope they didn't trip you up too much.

Cheers, Lilly xo

* * *

Terms

Biscuits - Crackers or cookies (could be either)

Boot - car trunk

Flat - apartment or condo

Mobile - cell phone

Nappy bag - diaper bag

Tea - used to describe either a hot beverage made from leaves, or the evening meal

Thongs - flip flops

Trolley - shopping basket

Unit - apartment or condo

ABOUT THE AUTHOR

Lilly Mirren is a USA Today Bestselling author. She lives in Brisbane, Australia with her husband and three children.

She always dreamed of being a writer and is now living that dream. When she's not writing, she's chasing her children or spending time with friends.

Her books combine heartwarming storylines with achingly realistic characters readers can't get enough of. Her debut series, The Waratah Inn, set in the delightful Cabarita Beach, hit the USA Today Bestseller list and since then, has touched the hearts of hundreds of thousands of readers across the globe.

Follow Lilly:

Website: www.lillymirren.com
Facebook: https://www.facebook.com/authorlillymirren/
Twitter: https://twitter.com/lilly_mirren
BookBub: https://www.bookbub.com/authors/lilly-mirren
Instagram: https://www.instagram.com/lilly_mirren/
Binge Books: https://bingebooks.com/author/lilly-mirren

Made in the USA
Monee, IL
05 March 2022